I0675609

THE LOST KEY OF BEING

by
Nan C. Cataldi

The Lost Key Of Being

THE LOST KEY OF BEING

by
Nan C. Cataldi

Cover Illustration by Mark Sean Wilson

The Lost Key Of Being

ISBN: 978-0-9883568-4-9

Library of Congress Control Number: 2015909969

Published by Inkwell Productions
10632 N. Scottsdale Rd, Unit 695
Scottsdale, AZ 85254-5280

Tel. 480-315-3781
E-mail info@inkwellproductions.com
Website www.inkwellproductions.com

Printed in the United States of America

The Lost Key Of Being

Table of Contents

The Lost Key Of Being

I would like to dedicate this book to my daughter, Stephanie, for all her help and encouragement. And to my handicapped son, Jeffrey, since he was my inspiration for Nicky.

I also want to thank my friends; Kathy W., Judy H., and Marian G. for believing in me and sticking by me for so many years.

CHAPTER 1

BEHIND THE VEIL

There is a secret world surrounding the planet Gaeya (Earth). It is hidden behind an invisible veil, called Wren, and ruled by the great and powerful Glymirra the Grand One. She is the Caretaker of the Living and Keeper of the Balance. After many eons Gaeya flourished, and Glymirra needed help to complete all the tasks required to maintain the stabilization of this celestial body, so a new species of spirit creatures was created to assist her. She called them Fae-rens. They were divided into the Woodland Fae-rens and the Sea Fae-rens. Each group was given two ranks: the helpers and the protectors. The helpers maintained Wren and assisted with all the creatures that lived there. The protectors were endowed with special powers of their own to protect all living creatures on Gaeya. Mated at creation, they are more powerful as a pair than separately. They also can transform into anything living, be it plant or animal, fish or bird. Given the orb of time that hangs suspended from their necks, these magical spirits can move swiftly on the wind and through time, if necessary, to protect, aiding animals in distress from flood, forest fires and earthquakes, sometimes providing sanctuary behind the veil when needed, until a terrible danger has passed. With the Fae-rens assistance, Gaeya prospered even more, and for many millenia, all lived in peace.

Then humans appeared on Gaeya. At first, they too, understood the importance of balance and harmony. However, being able to choose their life, as they were not bound by the the laws of Wren, Evil was able to possess them. They began to get greedy and jealous, fighting amongst themselves, and always taking more than they needed. Seeing the immense destruction and chaos on Gaeya, the Supreme of the Universe gave Glymirra the four Keys of Being. Each one is shaped like a three dimensional triangle: the Torka, a turquoise stone represents the five winds; Pera, a pearl stone symbolizing all the Seas; Gara, a garnet stone denoting Fire; and finally, the center stone, the Elka, an amber stone with a tiny leaf in the middle. It was the key of healing and re-birth. Together they would help Glymirra command the winds, the waters, fire, and re-birth of all creatures--except humans. She placed them in a secret underground grotto deep within the earth, contained in a triangular altar, to protect them until they were needed. Maintaining the harmony was important to the survival of all that existed on Gaeya.

It was in the human year of 1941, when A *Great War* took place. Mortal against mortal. Evil more powerful than ever imagined had taken over the land, trying to control not only all men but all that lived. This *dark power* began destroying everyone and everything that it came upon, including Glymirra's most trusted and most powerful leader of the Fae-rens, Phan-non, who was sent to spy on the Evil. Phan-non's destruction was a great loss to all that was good.

Glymirra, sensing the immensity of this sinister power, knew that if the Keys of Being were stolen or destroyed, all would be lost. So she hurried to the cavern alter, deep in the bowels of Gaeya and collected the four triangular keys from the grotto. Then, the Grand One placed them each in a small box made of oak and sealed them with golden wings. Next, she used her great powers to secure and close the entrance to the secret underground altar.

Upon returning to Wren with the boxes, Glymirra sent for her two strongest and most trusted protector Fae-rens:

Der-rex and Brin-dah. They were told to take the keys and hide them from this great Evil; To travel behind time and to distant lands to conceal them. The Fae-rens took the first key, the Torka, and hid it in a cave in the tenth century on an uninhabited island not far from Hawaii and protected it with much magic. The second key, the Pera, was concealed under the Great Barrier Reef off the coast of Australia and protected by the Sea Fae-rens. Gara, the third key was hidden on an island off the coast of Antarctica in an ice cave and also given heavy magical protection. Finally, the last and most important, the Elka, was concealed outside of time in a cave behind a waterfall, just inside the outer perimeter of Wren. Since no human could enter behind the Veil, except for an occasional human Guardian, who was carefully chosen by Glymirra, it would be safe there.

CHAPTER 2

REFLECTION OF AGES

Then in the human year of 1945, when the Evil had surrendered to the righteous, and the darkness was gone, it was time to return the Keys of Being to their proper place. Glymirra once again sent for her two most magical Fae-rens.

"It is time to restore the Keys to the Altar. We must heal this land," she said.

So again, the two set out on a journey to the far reaches of the land and behind time to recover them. When they finally reached the hiding place of the last, most important key, Der-rex and Brin-dah were startled to find an empty wooden box lying on the earth. The gold opulan, called the Watch of Wren, which was given to one of Glymirra's human Guardians, was lying on a large rock near the mystical ancient oak tree. They were too late! The key was gone! But how was that possible?

The two Fae-rens returned to Wren with the three keys and told Glymirra of finding the opulan and the empty wooden box that had housed the fourth key. The Grand One offered her hand, palm-up and asked Brin-dah to place the opulan into the center of her hand. She shut her large eyes, then slowly closed her hand around the gold disk. The Fae-rens watched with interest as their leader summoned her powers.

A few seconds later, Glymirra opened her bright eyes. Wearing a large grin on her face, she announced with a sigh of relief, " This opulan was not used by an evil being to enter behind the Veil. But we need to find out when the Elka was removed, who has taken it, and where it can be found. Please, sit." She pointed to a marble bench along the east wall of her chambers.

The two Fae-rens glided over to the bench and sat down. Their faces still showing concern about the loss of the Elka, they watched in silence as Glymirra immediately consulted the Reflection of Ages--a large, six-foot, diamond shaped, mirror-like, blue crystal that foretold the future and presented the past. It hung on the far wall of her chambers.

She closed her blue eyes and began to whisper in a strange language. Something began to happen to the crystal. Glymirra turned to the Far-ens, "Look. We will now be shown the day the day the Elka was taken."

The three of them watched as the very large crystal turned the deep blue color of a sapphire, then a thin mist appeared for a brief moment before clearing and revealing a mountain range in the Welsh countryside. It was early autumn, for the leaves on all the trees showed an array of red and yellow. There, at the foot of this small mountain, almost hidden from view by two large, old oak trees, stood a small stone cottage. A curl of smoke was rising out of its tiny chimney. Inside they saw a young mortal boy putting on a pair of brown, high-topped shoes with holes in the soles.

While he sat there tying up his shoes, he seemed to be in deep thought. Then without warning he jumped up and ran to an old wooden trunk at the bottom of a small cot-like bed. The trunk had thick iron straps wrapped around it that were held in place by large rivets. The young boy opened the heavy lid with great effort. Then he reached in and took out a red sack with a thin gold rope that held it closed. He began to untie the rope with much speed and put his hand inside to remove a solid gold disk with bird's wings etched on it. He smiled as he ran his fingers over the wings.

Glyimirra and the Fae-rens watched expectantly as the young boy twisted, turned and tried to pry the gold object open, but with no success.

"Pay close attention to this one. You will be able to hear some of the verbal exchanges along with some of his thoughts. This will give us more insight into the events of that day."

Then someone called out "Ian." The boy placed the disk on the bed and put on an over-sized jacket that was lying on a nearby chair. He turned toward the door, then paused to look once more at the gold disk. *I will show my cousin this special watch that grandfather gave me before he died. He told me it was a secret and to keep it safe. I know she will keep my secre*t, he thought as he grabbed it and put it into one of the large pockets of the jacket and hurried out of the cottage.

Outside, he met a young woman and an older boy. They talked for a few minutes. Then the young boy hugged the young woman. The older boy raised his hand and pointed towards a row of mountains nearby. Soon the three began to walk at a brisk pace toward a neighboring farm. They stopped there for a short time to see two new-born lambs and then continued on.

In no time they reached a waterfall. The two of them stopped briefly to watch as the water cascaded down the side if the mountain and flowed into the stream. The older boy spoke to the young woman, then both of them ran to the left side of the falls to view some strange, beautiful pink and purple flowers that were still blooming despite the chill of the autumn afternoon. The two of them smiled and laughed. The girl went over and smelled a large pink flower.

The younger boy lagged behind. He seemed to be enjoying all the beautiful sites, smiling and stopping every so often as he walked. Again thinking to himself, *I will miss this place.* Then he began to walk faster, and soon arrived at the foot of the waterfalls.

The young lad stopped and started to scan the area surrounding the falling water; he seemed to be searching for the others. Ian began to talk to himself. "Where are Sean and Victoria?" He turned his head left and right, looking for them. "What's that?"Something shiny flickered from the upper side of the rocky landscape, and he began to walk toward the glare which had peaked his curiosity. It led him to the right side of the falls. As he looked around for a way to climb the rocks , he found an old set of stone steps obscured by foliage. He pushed some of the bushes aside and began to climb them, forgetting all about Sean and Victoria.

Soon he reached a ledge with many quartz rocks laying on the earthen surface. The young boy's face lit-up with excitement. *Wow, these will be great for my rock collection.* Ian took a moment to remember his grandfather. It was his grandfather that showed him the landscape and taught him about the link between all the living. Each plant and animal has a purpose. All must co-exist to help the other thrive. That's when he began collecting rocks and leaves. Humans must learn to share with all the other living things on Earth to maintain the balance. Ian wasn't sure what that was, his learning was cut short by the death of his grandfather. He had to stop day-dreaming, so he shook his head and again began to look at the sparkling rocks.

He picked up two large, white quartz rocks, examined them, and then dropped them into his pocket. He walked a little closer to the rocky wall and noticed a narrow opening in the rock. A grin and look of interest showed on his face as Glymirra and her Fae-rens watched him enter a strange glittering cave. A ray of setting sun showed through a thin crack in the wall of the cave. It seemed to light up the back of the cave. The boy's eyes widened as he looked down and saw many pieces of shiny quartz all around his feet. *I can not believe it, look at all these*, he thought. Then he picked up two specimens and put them in the other pocket. Ping! A frightened look came over him. Immediately he put his hand in his right pocket and pulled out the gold disk. He turned it over and over looking for any damage. Then he let out a sigh.

As the young boy held it in his hand, the disk began to glow, and without warning, it opened up. He squinted, trying to see what was inside, but it was too dark near the opening of the cave. So, he held the disk out-stretched in the palm of his hand and began to walk slowly toward the light at the back of the cave. The light became a blinding brilliance, as it bounced off a wall of solid crystal quartz. It was so bright that the boy shaded his eyes with his other hand.

Then the hand holding the disk began to vibrate and glow a bright orange color. Whoosh! The young boy was suddenly floating on a puffy, white cloud. In less than a second, the cloud was gone and he was now standing in front of a field of huge ferns and strange massive, yellow flowers that resembled sunflowers, which towered ten or twelve feet into the air.

As the Fae-rens continued to watch, the boy's face seemed to flush with shock and fear. He stood still for several minutes, looking confused. Then taking in a deep breath, he began walking placing one foot in front of the other, as if with great caution, heading down a narrow path toward a huge, shining, ancient oak tree.

Soon the boy was standing a few yards from the front of the fifty foot high oak tree. He looked up and down at the tree, amazed at it's size. The trunk was about fifteen feet in circumference. It radiated much light. As he drew closer he realized that it's leaves were made of gold and tiny wooden boxes hung off the tree's limbs.

"Oh no," Brin-dah cried. "The boy has breached our magical protection and entered behind the veil."

"It's alright, Brin-dah," Glymirra said as she smiled. "That is the Guardian Timothy McWilliams's opulan. The young human is his grandson, Ian. Timothy died before he could pass the knowledge of our realm and the purpose of his guardianship to him. He only had time to teach him the importance of environmental harmony. The young boy did not know what he possessed. It was only by mere coincidence that he found the cavern and happened upon the portal just at the proper moment. Even having the opulan would not have opened the doorway, because they only open once every three days for a short time. As you saw, the young one was very surprised, even frightened. Now, let us continue watching the rest of that day in the Reflection of Ages."

Glyimirra and the two Fae-rens continued to watch as Ian set the gold disk on top of the smaller of two nearby boulders. Then he walked around the trunk of the tree twice, repeatedly jumping up and stretching his arms toward the lower branches, trying to grab on to one of them. But soon he realized he could not reach any of the branches. He looked very frustrated.

Finally, the boy walked over to the larger boulder that sat next to the tree. He touched the rough edges of the boulder with his hands. He smiled as he placed one foot up into a groove on the side of the rock and began to climb it. In no time at all, he reached the top. The young one stood up and touched a nearby limb. He began to climb up the branch, stopping to grab a wooden box off of it. He carefully opened it but found nothing inside. He shook his head left and right, then dropped the tiny empty box. It fell to the ground. He looked around, climbed a little higher, and grabbed another box off a larger branch. He opened it and found it to be empty also.

Once again the boy surveyed the branches of the tree, until he spied a box with something shiny and gold on it. He decided to climb closer to that particular box, reaching up he pulled it off the branch. He took it in his hand, running a finger over the gold wings that sealed the opening. Looking excited, he tried to open the box. The boy made contorted faces as he tugged, pushed, and twisted the lid, but it did not open. He paused for a moment, took in a deep breath and gave the lid one last, forceful tug. It finally opened. His eyes became larger and a huge smile appeared across his face. Inside he found a beautiful brownish-yellow gem stone. He took it out of the box to get a closer look, turning it over and over in his hand. It was strange-looking, shaped like a crystal prism, and enclosed in the center was a tiny green leaf.

All of a sudden, he jerked his head up, as a young woman's voice shouted, "Ian, where are you? It will be dark soon. We must go."

The boy appeared so startled that he dropped the box and almost lost his hold on the branch. Without much thought, he shoved the amber gem stone into his pocket and began to climb down the tree. When he reached the bottom, he stood for a moment looking at his surroundings and touching his pocket where his new treasure lay, making sure he had not lost it on the way down. Soon fear showed on his face. He seemed lost. He turned all around looking for the way back and decided to walk down the path away from the tree toward the large ferns and the mammoth yellow flowers he first encountered.

Again a voice called "Ian." So he began walking toward the voice.

Whoosh! All at once, he found himself back in the cave. His face flushed again in alarm, as he looked around and realized he had left the gold disk on the small boulder next to the ancient oak tree. In a panic, Ian turned back and began feeling that solid wall of the quartz with his hands, touching and hitting it, trying to find a way to open it again. He yelled, "N-o-o-o-o! I must get grandfather's watch!" However, the secret opening had disappeared, along with the clouds and the ancient oak tree.

The young boy seemed to become very upset and defeated. Sweat beaded up on his brow, and he leaned heavily against the cave wall. As he rested, once again a loud, female voice yelled, "Ian, where are you. It's getting late. Please, answer me?" This time there was fear in her voice. He began to hurry toward the front of the cave, but paused as his face flushed once more and a feeling of sadness came over him like a dark cloud. He realized that he had lost the last special present his grandfather had entrusted to him. The gold, watch-like, disk could never be replaced. Sulking, he reached the cave opening, and yelled, "Here I am," as he started running down the steps toward the young woman.

"Sorry," the lad whispered as he hung his head in despair. The older boy joined them as they made their way back to the cottage.

When the three of them arrived at the cottage, they were met by an older woman who scolded them for being so late. She told the boys to finish packing their trunks.

"Uncle has brought you boys some new jackets to wear

on our voyage, so pack your old ones. We leave first thing in the morning," the woman said.

The young boy hung his head in grief at the loss of the gold disk and walked into his room. He picked up the empty red sack sitting on his bed, looked at it and began to cry. As tears ran down his cheeks, he whispered, "I am so sorry, grandfather. You trusted me with your special watch, and I lost it." Forgetting all about the amber crystal gemstone he found and had placed into his pocket, he opened the trunk, took the red sack and the old jacket he was wearing and set them in the trunk then slowly closed the lid.

"Now I understand." Glymirra looked at Brin-dah and Der-rex, then said "The Elka has traveled in that old trunk with this boy to another part of Gaeya. I will again ask the Reflection of Ages where you must go to find it and return it to me."

The Grand One closed her eyes once more and whispered, when the mist cleared, a desert-like land shown in the crystal mirror, then it was gone, and a wooden trunk with large iron slats appeared. It sat in a dark and dusty room, between several other boxes.

"This is the house of Ian McWilliams. The trunk is in the attic of the abode."

"But Grand One, you know we cannot enter there. It is our law that we must not enter an occupied human's dwelling, lest we lose our powers and turn to stone," Brin-dah said with a terrified look on her face. Then she turned to Der-rex for support. He, too, looked frightened.

Glymirra, seeing their anxiety, replied, "Do not despair, there are always other ways."

Once again The Grand One consulted the supernatural crystal. "I need to know when the wooden and iron box with the Elka will leave this dwelling and who will be the one to retrieve the Key. "She again closed her eyes and whispered words unknown to the Fae-rens.

The crystal mirror misted over once more to reveal a boy lifting an old jacket out of a wooden trunk. As he put on the jacket, a faint yellow glow could be seen coming from one of it's pockets.

"This mortal child must be found and protected. He will obtain the Elka and you two will get it from him and return it to me. I will check the time line to find out when, but you will need to go as soon as possible to the future. With the balance off, all on Gaeya are in danger, not only from the elements, but from the rapid-growing Evil which is feeding off of all the planet's catastrophic events. Wait here."

Glymirra left Brin-dah and Der-rex, but soon returned with a tiny hourglass. "Take this," she said, as she handed it to Brin-dah, who then placed it into the pocket of her knee length toga. "This will help you narrow down the time you have to find and make contact with the boy." Glyimirra waved her hand over their orbs. " Your orbs will take you to the desert land, in the future, where the boy lives. You must bring me the Elka. Go now and be safe."

CHAPTER 3

THE STRANGE LITTLE DOG
SEVENTY YEARS IN THE FUTURE

A strong, warm wind passed in front of the school bus door just as Nicky Kirkland was about to disembark. It blew his cap off, and he stared with a look of disbelief. It made him pause, then he slowly stepped down to the sidewalk. He was a handsome boy of almost ten, with big dark brown eyes, long curly eyelashes like a girl, smooth, light complexion, and dark brown wavy hair that always stuck out of one of his caps. His frame was thin, and he was slightly tall for his age. A noticeable limp distracted from his good looks, which became apparent as he walked over to pick up his hat. Most adults took an immediate liking to Nicky's innocent ways and easy-going disposition, but his peers made fun of him and sometimes bullied him.

As he started walking toward home, he heard a noise, looked over his shoulder, and noticed a small, brown dog following him. The dog barked and Nicky turned around. "Hey boy, are you l-lost? Where's your collar? Are you h-hungry?" The dog sat down and stared at him. Nicky took off his backpack and sat down on the sidewalk next to him. He unzipped the front pocket of the bag and pulled out some peanut butter crackers. Nicky put two crackers in the palm of his hand and stretched his arm out to the dog. The timid animal snatched the crackers from Nicky's hand and gobbled them up. Nicky reached over to pet the dog but never got the chance. As soon as his hand was an inch from petting its head, the little dog stood up, turned, and ran as fast as his legs could move, disappearing into thin air just before reaching the next street. "Whoa!" Nicky stood up with a puzzled look on his face. He had never seen a small dog move so fast. *Where did he go? It was like magic.* Nicky stood there for a moment staring at the direction the dog had run. He rubbed his eyes in disbelief. Then he shrugged his shoulders, grabbed his backpack, and again started for home.

Soon the boy arrived at the small stucco rancher on the corner of 15th and Cactus Flower Lane. Nicky lived there with his mother Claire. They had moved to Arizona ten months ago from Virginia. Nicky walked up the driveway to the front door. As he inserted his key, he heard the whining of his dog, Punkin. She couldn't wait to see Nicky. She jumped up at him as soon as the door opened. Nicky grabbed the leash that was hanging by the door, attached it to her collar, and off they went.

The two of them walked across the street to Mr. Rosanelli's to check-in. Claire asked Mr. R., as Nicky called him, to look out for Nicky until she came home from work. He was a nice, elderly man that spent most of his days close to home. Claire worked at the nearby Urgent Care Center usually until 4:30 pm, but some days she wouldn't get home until 5:30 pm.

When Nicky arrived at the house, Mr. R. was outside pruning his bushes. He looked up as Nicky and Punkin walked over.

"So Nick, how was your last day of school?"

"It was okay, Mr. R. But I am glad we are done for w-w-winter break. School's t-too much work." Nicky sighed, in disgust.

"Nicky, did you hear that Molly is going to be staying with Mrs. Grey for a few weeks? I know you don't have anyone here in this old neighborhood to hangout with, so now you can hangout with her. Isn't that the phrase kids use now-a-days?"

"Yeah. It will be f-fun. Molly's c-cool ," he replied. " I'm going to take Punkin home. Mum wanted me to w-water that small patch of grass in the backyard. See ya." Nicky waved goodbye and headed back across the street.

When they first moved to Arizona, Nicky was very lonely. He didn't spend time with anyone from school. He found it difficult to make friends with kids his own age. Most of the guys at school ignored him, since he was unable to play sports, and some laughed at his stuttering. So when he wasn't in school, he spent most of his days at home playing video games, putting together jigsaw puzzles, playing with his dog, or doing the chores his mother gave him. Soon he was befriended by an old man, his neighbor Mr. Rosanelli, the Neighborhood Watch policeman Officer Montoya or Monty as Nicky called him, and now Molly, who sometimes visited. She was the nine-year-old granddaughter of Mrs. Grey, who lived next door to Mr. R.

After putting away the leash and giving Punkin a treat, Nicky went out the sliding glass doors to the backyard. He took the garden hose off the patio, unraveled it, hooked it to the faucet and turned on the water. Meanwhile, Punkin whined as she looked out the glass door at Nicky.

"Stop that, Punkin," Nicky yelled. "You know you can't c-come out here when I water the grass. Mum would be really upset if you got m-mud on her carpet." Punkin stopped whining but sat at the door watching Nicky's every move.

All of a sudden, to Nicky's surprise, the hose went limp and the nozzle turned toward him with leering, black narrow eyes. Nicky screamed and threw the hose down. Punkin jumped up and down, barking and growling at the door, upset that she couldn't help. But then the snake-like hose rose up from the ground standing as tall as Nicky. It turned into a large-hooded cobra, faced him, hissed and disappeared leaving the hose lying on the grass.

Mr. Rosenelli was still working outside when he heard Nicky's loud scream. He hurried across the street to check on Nicky. When he arrived the boy was staring at the hose that lay on the ground and his body was shaking.

"What happened, Nick? I heard you cry out. Are you okay?"

Nicky took a minute to answer him. " I-I thought the h-hose turned into a sn-snake and hissed at me."

"It looks like a regular garden hose to me," said Mr. Rosenelli, looking a little concerned.

"I know. I g-guess I was s-seeing things."

"Are you sure you are alright?"

"Yea. I'll just put the h-hose away and go inside and wait for m-mum."

"Well, if you need me, Nicky, I'll be home."

"Thanks, Mr. R."

Still a little shaken, Nicky went inside the house. Punkin immediately went over to him and began to lick his hands. "Come on girl, let's g-go into the den and put a game in my XBOX. I need to c-calm down." He sat for a moment then he looked at Punkin , "I'll play this until m-mum gets home. Then I'll feed you. Okay girl?" Punkin came and laid beside his chair. Nicky played his video game while the two of them awaited Claire's arrival.

It was almost 5:00 pm when Punkin began to bark. Then Nicky heard the garage door open and his mother's car alarm gave a loud beep. He and Punkin hurried to the door to greet her. Punkin sat at the door and waited for some acknowledgment from her mistress. Claire hung-up her keys on the hook by the door and turned to pat the dog's head. Punkin's tail wagged with excitement as she followed Claire into the kitchen.

"What's for dinner, Mum? I'm h-hungry," Nicky spouted. He seemed to have put the hose incident out of his mind and was back to normal.

Claire opened the freezer searching for something quick and appealing. "How about hot dogs for dinner?"

"Sure, Mum. Hey, guess what?"

"What is it, Nicky?"

"Well when I was coming home from school this little d-d-dog followed me. I think he was a hot dog or a w-wiener dog. He had short little legs, but he could r-run r-really fast. When I turned around to pet him, he just d-disappeared. It...it was weird, almost like m-magic."

Claire turned to Nicky smiling, "You have such an active imagination."

"No, Mum it's true." But Nicky would not tell her about the hose changing into a snake. He was not sure it really happened. He would keep that incident to himself.

Claire raised her brow and changed the subject. "So, are you excited about school being out for the holiday?"

"Yeah, Mum."

Claire went back to her room to change for dinner. Right away Punkin cornered Nicky, so he went to the cupboard and pulled out a package of dog food, opened it and put it into Punkin's dish. She wouldn't let him forget her.

Dinner was soon ready. Nicky downed two hot dogs and two helpings of beans in a few minutes. Claire glared at him in amazement. Nicky's eyes met hers .

"What, Mum? I told you I-I was h-hungry!"

"When I finish, would you like to go to the corner store

with me?"

"Sure, Mum." Shopping was one of Nicky's favorite things to do.

Soon, they headed over to Walt's Shop and Pharmacy that was on the corner. Claire parked the car. Just as the two of them got out, a big ,warm gust of wind passed them, knocking off Nicky's cap. Nicky stopped and thought for a moment. *That's twice today.* Then he hobbled over and picked up his hat, dusted it off and placed it back on his head. Claire looked over at Nicky and then started walking toward the door. She noticed a small, young, red-haired, homeless woman dressed in a dirty, long-sleeved, yellow tee-shirt, worn jeans, and flip-flops. She was leaning against the wall next to the entrance. It was a cool evening, but the woman did not seem cold; she only looked tired and helpless. The young woman was holding a small brown bundle in her arms. It moved, and a little head with floppy ears popped-up. Nicky noticed that the head belonged to the little dog he had seen earlier, and said, "Hey, so that's your d-dog. He followed me part way home today. Boy, he sure can r-run." The woman looked up and stared at him but said nothing. Feeling sorry for the young woman, Claire opened her purse, pulled out five dollars and gave it to her.

"I hope this will help." The woman took the money but

gave no response and kept her head down.

Nicky stood impatiently holding the door. "Mum...come on." Claire turned and they walked into the store.

As soon as they entered the store, the small, young woman looked down at her dog and whispered, "You are right Der-rex, he is the one foretold to us by the Reflection of Ages. I sense that he has not yet acquired the Elka. I will leave soon to seek the guidance of Glyimirra and bring back the sentinels to guard him. He and the key will need to be protected. I know we have taken every precaution, but the growing evil still feels very close."

Just then another warm gust of wind passed by, and she and the dog were gone.

Nicky and Claire walked down the beverage aisle and picked up a few bottles of water. Then Claire headed over to the Pharmacy to pick up a prescription. When she turned around, Nicky was gone. Looking around she walked over to the toy aisle .

"Nicky, I just need one more thing ,so please stay with me."

"Ah, Mum, I…I wanted to get a new puzzle."

"Not today," Claire said with her eyebrows raised. Your birthday is tomorrow."

"Ycah! I can't w-wait!" Nicky's face lit-up and his eyes

began to twinkle.

As they came out of the store, Claire stopped and looked for the young woman and her dog. But they were gone...almost as if they'd never been there. Claire shook her head to clear the thought, and the two of them got in the car to head home.

That night about 9:00 PM, Punkin went running to the window in the small living room, pushing the curtain open with her nose. She began to growl and bark into the night. She seemed very upset. Claire was taking a bath, when she heard all the barking, so she asked Nicky to check on Punkin. Nicky hurried out of his bedroom to see what was upsetting the dog. He pushed her away from the window and peered out, but Punkin kept barking. "There is nothing outside girl. C-c-calm down." But Punkin kept pacing and snarled a few more times. Then as fast as she had started barking, the dog settled down.

"Nicky...What was it?" Claire hollered.

"Nothing, Mum," Nicky responded. He looked at Punkin. "You're a silly dog."

But the dog sensed the invisible eyes watching and heard the magical, calming whispers that only she could hear and understand, for outside the living room window, hiding behind the bushes, two, small, invisible Fae-rens sat.

The female reached into her tunic and pulled out an

ancient hour glass. Examining it closely, she said, "Look Der-rex. According to the timeline from the Reflection of Ages, he will retrieve the Elka in less than three sunsets. I must leave you now. It is important that I meet with Glymirra and bring the Sentinels to guard both of them. They will accompany me on my return. In my absence, you must look after the boy." She shivered slightly. Then she looked again into Der-rex eyes and said, "I feel the evil. It is very close, now. You will need help, till my return. You know that our interference with humans is limited, so you must seek out a human helper, especially since we do not have a Guardian in this land. I know that Glymirra has used other humans besides the Guardians in times of great need. Maybe there is someone that is close to the boy that may be able to help. Look inside his mind and see."

Then Brin-dah touched the small blue orb that magically hung in the air around her neck, and with a great gust of warm, swirling wind, she was gone, traveling on the wind and back in time to seek the wisdom of The Grand One.

CHAPTER 4

THE BIRTHDAY

Nicky opened his big brown eyes one at a time. Something wet had touched his cheek. As he turned his head in the opposite direction, a dark brown curl fell into his face. It was his morning wake up call. His dog Punkin would lick and nudge until he acknowledged her. But it was the first day of winter break and he did not need to get-up early.

"Get out. Leave me alone." Nicky yelled in a sleepy manner. Nicky had a very disturbing night's sleep. First he couldn't sleep because he was excited about his birthday, he would be ten in the morning, old enough to have his own cell phone. But then his dreams became nightmares. Large snake eyes and evil hissing kept waking him up. It left him feeling very worn out.

"Come on, girl. Let's go out," he heard his mother say.

Punkin ran down the hallway to the kitchen, and sat down by the side door, her tail wagging with excitement. Claire took the red leash that hung on a hook by the kitchen door and secured it to Punkin's collar. Then they went outside for their morning stroll. As they left, the wind caught the door, and it closed with a loud slam.

Nicky sat up with a jolt, yawning, as he yelled, "Mum, don't slam the d-door." But she didn't hear him. He saw the large calendar that was taped to his closet door with today's date circled. He screamed at the top of his lungs "Hey, today is my birthday! Yeah, awesome," he hollered again in an elated voice. He jumped into his slippers and hurried down the hallway to the kitchen.

"Yeah! It's m-my birthday, happy b-birthday to me," as he sang to himself. He was now ten. "I'm g-getting a cell phone!" He attempted to jump as he screamed it, smiling from ear to ear.

Upon entering the kitchen, he opened cupboard after cupboard, lifting up dishes and spices. He then opened the drawers, going through the flatware.

"Where are they?" he asked himself. *Where can they be?* he thought, as he opened the pantry door. Disappointed, he walked into the small dining room, pulled out a chair and sat down.

Mum would always have a special breakfast and some presents waiting for me, he thought. *It's my birthday. I don't understand.* He sat there pouting and pondering.

A few minutes later, Claire entered with their dog. She took the leash off the dog, and Punkin ran over to Nicky, sat down, panting and wagging her tail, waiting for her young master to pet her.

Nicky pushed her away. "Leave me alone, Punkin," he sulked.

"What's wrong, Nicky?" his mother asked. It was rare to see Nicky unhappy.

"Well, where's my c-c-cake and my presents?"

Claire chuckled. "You are a young man now, I think you can wait till I get home from work." Nicky turned to face his mother, looking at her with very disappointed eyes.

She came over to Nicky, kissed him on top of his head and said, "Happy Birthday, my little man."

"Don't call me little. I'm almost as t-tall as you, Mum. Besides I-I am older...like you said," Nicky piped-in.

Claire looked at her son and smiled." I have to go to work, but I'll take you out for dinner and give you your presents later."

She felt guilty leaving him on his birthday. This was a happy, as well as a very sad day. She always made his birthday extra special since the car accident four years ago on his birthday that had injured Nicky and changed both their lives.

"Did you get me the c-cell phone I wanted? Everyone at s-school has one."

"I'm sorry, Nicky. You'll just have to wait. I'm running behind, and I don't want to be late."

"Did you get m-me the new Magic Battle-Star v-v-video game?"

Claire just grinned, then poured some coffee into her silver travel mug, put the top on, and set it on the counter. She grabbed the rest of her things and proceeded toward the door .

"Can I go to the thrift store today?" Nicky asked. "I want to go and...look...for...a...new puzzle." Nicky said in a long drawn-out statement.

"Do you have money to go?"

"No-o-o-o-o...", was the sheepish reply.

Claire opened her small black leather purse, reached into the side pocket, and pulled out two five dollar bills. She handed them to Nicky and said "Since, it's your birthday, here's ten dollars. But you have to finish your chores first. Please check the list on the fridge."

"But it's my b-birthday. Why do I have to do chores?"

"Because you are a young man now and if you want a cell phone, you must be more responsible."

"Okay, I get it," Nicky responded in a disappointed tone.

"Now, I really have to run." She kissed Nicky on the cheek, took the keys off the hook near the door, and looking back at him, she smiled. "I'll be home at 4:30, ok?"

"Yeah, Mum," he said, rolling his eyes.

"Don't forget to be ready!"

"I won't!" he exclaimed as he wrinkled up his nose.

Claire hurried into the garage. *Click, click* She opened the car door, threw her purse and lunchbox in the seat next to her, and climbed into the car. The garage door opened with a rumble.

Nicky heard the car door slam and the engine rev. Just then, he noticed his mother's coffee mug sitting on the counter. He grabbed it, and hurried out the front door after her, shouting, "Wait." But it was too late. The garage door rolled down and Nicky's eyes caught the back of the silver car as it turned the corner. With a sigh, he went back into the house.

The excitement of the day returned to him. He dressed in a hurry, putting on blue jeans, his favorite, white Nascar t-shirt with his favorite driver's car on it, and his black and white tennis shoes. He finished his chores in less than fifteen minutes.

I have $10 to spend, he thought. Nicky's favorite thing was to shop for baseball caps and puzzles at the Goodmart located at the small plaza four blocks from his home. He grabbed his orange Velcro wallet, *rrrriiiip* was the sound it made as he opened it and slipped the ten dollars in the bill section and tucked it into his back pocket. He grabbed his denim jacket that laid at the bottom of his newly-made bed, and put on one of his favorite caps. Then he took his keys off the top of the small dresser that sat across from his bed and headed down the hall to the front door. Looking back at Punkin, Nicky said, "I'll be back, girl. Be good!" Then he locked the door and began his jaunt to the thrift store.

Since moving away from his friends, going to the small plaza to shop was a way to be around people. He had even made friends with some of the workers there. Nicky got more excited with each step as he got closer to his goal: the Goodmart Thrift Store. Shopping was always a fun time. He especially liked going to this particular thrift store, because they always had really neat things and they were cheap. He could spend two or three hours deciding what treasures to purchase with his money. He was always friendly, saying hello to various neighbors as he made his way to the intersection where the store was located. But today, he was met by three older boys, who went to his school and rode his bus.

"Hey Gimpy, wh-where are you go-go-goin'?" one of the boys said, mimicking Nicky's stutter. Then all three of them started to laugh. They liked to make fun of Nicky. One of them even threw some gravel at him. A chubby man that was washing his car in his driveway saw Nicky duck and cover his face as he was showered with gravel. The man shouted, "You boys better stop throwing stuff at that kid or I'll tell your parents." The boys looked at each other, then took off running down the next street.

"Thanks, Mister." Nicky yelled and waved to the man. His good mood returned as he continued his trek to the store.

The light was red when Nicky approached the corner. Today he stood with great impatience waiting for the walk sign to appear. He was just so overwhelmed with the thought of shopping for his own birthday present . When the light changed at the busy intersection, he cautiously entered the crosswalk. As soon as he made sure there were no cars coming, he hurried to the other side of the street, with marked limping as he was very eager to make it to his destination.

As he walked into the Goodmart, Nicky's face lit-up.

Ten dollars could buy two puzzles or a sweatshirt. Today he wanted something special. He was more excited than usual, walking up and down the aisles.

He heard an associate say "Hey, Nick, how's it goin'?"

Nicky waved and in a loud, cheerful voice replied, " It's my ***birthday.***" Then with a huge grin on his face he proceeded to the electronics area, where there was an array of used radios and stereos, but nothing appealed to him. He continued to walk down some more aisles until he reached the clothing section. A bright, blue t-shirt caught his eye. It had another race car on the front. He pulled it out of the rack, but noticed it was the wrong size, so he put it back. Frowning, he looked through a few more shirts, pulling each one out to exam it closer.

Then he heard someone whistling a short distance away. He looked around to see a short, pudgy, gray-haired man, wearing thick glasses, coming up the side aisle carrying an old wooden box with iron slats around it. It was Sam, the assistant manager. Nicky hung-up the shirt he was holding and started following him.

"Hey, Sam, what's in that w-wooden box?" he asked with great enthusiasm. The trunk was like a magnet pulling Nicky closer. There seemed to be a slight glow emanating from it. Curiosity took over, he had to see what was in it.

"Just some clothes that the McWilliams family donated when their grandfather died. You know Nicky, Ian McWilliams is kind of famous. He emigrated to the United States, after World War II and became a renowned conservationist and environmentalist. He helped establish some of our country's national forests. He wanted his clothes to be donated since he was always giving to the community. Our store received three boxes and this old trunk today from his estate. I haven't looked through any of them yet. Would you like to look with me?"

Nicky's eyes grew big. "Y*eah*! Thanks, Sam."

Sam leaned toward Nicky and whispered, " Just don't tell anyone. It's our secret."

"Okay," Nicky whispered back.

Sam set the trunk down on a large chair. Then he opened the lid. Nicky peered in and began to lift clothes out of it. "Hey, Sam, look at this funny hat." He pulled out a brown and green plaid cap. It had a flat front and baggy-looking back. It was large and fell over his eyes when he tried it on.

Sam laughed and said, "You know, Nicky, some of these clothes are very old. They look like some of the things my grandfather wore from the 1940s."

"Really, Sam? Like this old jacket?" Nicky took it out

and held it up to his chest. Then he turned it around toward himself and looked at the large pockets. "Hey, Sam, can I have this old jacket ? I think it's r-really cool and awesome." Nicky took the jacket and put it on. "See, it even fits," he said as he stood there modeling it.

Sam stood looking at Nicky, with an eyebrow raised, grinning, not saying a word. "Well, its almost f-fits. Mum said I'm still growing. So I c-can grow into it, okay?"

"Okay, Nicky. You've convinced me." Sam chuckled. "I'll give you that old brown jacket for five dollars."

"Hey, that's great! I still have five dollars to spend."

"Maybe you can buy that old plaid hat, too" Sam said smiling from ear to ear.

"Na-a-a. Quit...t-t-teasing me, Sam. Do you have any used ball caps today?"

"I don't think we've gotten any more in. Come back Tuesday or Wednesday, we might have some then. But look around. Maybe you'll find something special to go with your new jacket."

"Thanks, Sam." Nicky's face shined with delight as he left, carrying his new old jacket.

He began to stroll down the toy aisle. He picked up a game. He took the lid off, pulled out a few pieces and shook his head. Then he set it back on the shelf. He looked some more but nothing caught his eye. He decided to go to the check-out and pay for his jacket.

The clerk took the jacket and flipped it around and around, looking for the price tag. Just then Sam came over and told him. "It's five dollars. I haven't had a chance to put the tag on it yet."

"Thanks, Sam. Now I can ring you up young man," the middle-aged, female clerk told Nicky.

The boy pulled the orange velcro wallet from his pocket. He was so excited as he took out one five dollar bill and laid it on the counter. The jacket was placed in a large plastic bag and handed to Nicky with his receipt. He just could not wait to wear it, so he stopped by the door, took it out of the bag and switched jackets, putting his good jacket into the bag. A huge smile lit up his face as he walked out of the store.

Nicky began walking home as fast as his legs could move, making his limp more apparent. He was so thrilled with his new purchase that he could not stop smiling. *I cannot wait to show Mum and Mr. Rosenelli my new jacket*, he thought to himself, as he started toward home. But a strange thing happened, the beautiful day turned cloudy and the wind began to pick-up. Then a big, chilling gust of wind blew off his cap. Nicky stopped, picked up his cap and put it in the bag with his jacket. He didn't want it to blow away. The wind blew harder and harder, and the few clouds multiplied and turned dark and scary. The black clouds that rolled in, now covered the entire sky. Suddenly there was a loud clap of thunder. Nicky jumped. Then he saw the sky light up from a huge bolt of lightening. He had to hurry home. But the cold wind blew harder, pushing against him with such force that he made little progress. The thunder clapped louder, and the lightening was so bad and so frequent that the sky looked like large flashing, flood lights. One of the huge, angry-looking black clouds seemed to be following Nicky.

Nicky was very confused. It was like a huge monsoon was coming, but this was winter time. Then, without warning, the cloud burst open above him, and hail as big as golf balls rained down on him, stinging his head and hands. He began to wish that he could run. He needed to get home. As he limped down the sidewalk he had to duck to avoid being hit by bending tree branches and debris flying in the harsh wind. Behind one of the trees that ran along the side walk, Der-rex sat. In a low voice, he said "I must use my magic. There is no time to get help. I must protect the boy. He now is in possession of the Elka! Brin-dah should be back soon with the Sentinels."

To Nicky's surprise a sharp warm gust of wind swirled

under Nicky's feet, lifting him up a few inches off the ground. He began to feel strange, almost like he was walking on air. And before he knew it, he was at Cactus Lane. Just as he turned into his driveway, a bolt of lightening hit the neighbor's tree, and a large branch came crashing to the ground, nearly hitting Nicky as he leaped out of the way. His face went pale with horror. He pulled out his key and hurried to the door. He could hear the hail pounding the roofs of the surrounding houses. His heart was racing and his breathing was rapid. He was so frightened and shaking that he could barely get the key in the door. He could hear Punkin whining inside.

The key at last found its way into the lock. He turned the knob as fast as he could and opened the door. Then Nicky hurried into the house and slammed the door shut. He dropped to the floor, leaning up against the inside of the door, and sat there until his heart and breathing slowed down. "Boy, th-that was a close...close one, girl" he said to Punkin as he hugged her. At the next moment, a very loud, long, raging clap of thunder rang in his ears. It sounded as if a man was screaming with fury. Then...everything stopped. As swiftly as it had started, the storm ended.

Nicky peeked out the window a few minutes later and saw that the sun was shining once more. He could see no left over remnants of the hail, and the tree limb that broke off near him, had disappeared. He was again baffled. *Did the storm really happen? What is going on? Should I tell Mum? No, I don't want to scare her. Besides I can't prove anything. I guess I should try to forget about it.*

He waited and played with Punkin until 4:00 pm. Then Nicky hurried into the shower, cleaned up and dressed for his birthday dinner. Claire arrived at 4:30 pm. Nicky heard the car alarm and ran to open the door for her. Claire entered, carrying two packages wrapped in race car paper. She smiled as she handed them to Nicky and gave him a big hug.

"Happy Birthday, my little man."

"Quit, calling me that, Mum!"

She laughed. "Let me get out of my uniform and into party clothes." as she headed toward her bedroom. Nicky used great speed in unwrapping the two presents. One was the video game he wanted, and the other was a model of a race car.

"Thanks, Mum!" he yelled.

Claire hollered back" When I get paid again, we'll look at getting you a cell phone."

"Really, Mum?"

"Really, Nicky."

"Wow! This is the b-best b-birthday ever!" Then he

remembered his new/old jacket and became excited all over again.

Nicky couldn't wait for Claire to come out of her bedroom so he happily began telling her about his new/old coat through the door.

"When you come out I'll p-put it on for you."

A few minutes later Claire emerged all ready to go for dinner. Just then Nicky stood in front of her wearing an ugly, brown, oversized jacket. It smelled musty and looked very old.

"Whoa, Nick! You really like this...uh...jacket?" She asked very perplexed.

"It's c-cool and it...it has these awesome pockets. Look." He put his hands in the left front pocket and turned like a model. Then he pulled out two sparkling rocks, looking at them in wonder. " Wow, Mum! Look at these! I just found some c-cool looking r-rocks in this pocket." Smiling he asked "Do you like my new jacket ?"

Claire stood looking at him for a minute. She would never hurt his feelings by telling him no. "Yeah Nicky. It's different, and you have some...uh...nice...rocks, and just look at those huge pockets."

"I know it's a little b-big, Mum, but you said I'm still g-growing, right?"

"Yes," Claire said as she nodded and smiled. "It's getting late. We need to go, Nicky," Claire stated, as she headed for the door. So he ran back to his room, placing the rocks from his left pocket on his dresser. Then he reached his hand into the right pocket and found some more rocks. Not even looking at them, he set them also on the dresser. Then he took off his new/old jacket and threw it on the bed.

Claire called down the hall, "Come on, Nicky, I'm getting hungry!"

Nicky grabbed his denim jacket, pulled on a cap, then eagerly limped over to the door and off the two of them went to George's Bar-B-Que for his Birthday dinner.

Two hours later they returned home. Nicky couldn't wait to play his new video game with space lasers and protective shields. Punkin joined him in the den while he played. Claire watched the news in the small living room. Another earthquake hit China, causing much destruction, and a hurricane flooded parts of eastern Australia; a volcano that had been sleeping for a thousand years erupted in Italy. There were so many natural disasters of late, even the scientists were stumped by the changes in the earth over the last two decades.

At ten Claire and Nicky retired for the night. Punkin joined Nicky and curled up at the bottom of his bed. It was such a great day that he could not stop dreaming of cell phones, video games, old jackets and even of a strange yellow glow coming from the top of his dresser. Everything seemed so real to him that he woke-up smiling, sat up and looked around his room, laid down again and fell back to sleep.

CHAPTER 5

THE BEWITCHED DOG

The next afternoon the doorbell rang. Punkin began to bark. Nicky went to the door and yelled, "Who is it?"

"It's me, Molly."

Nicky opened the door and there in front of him stood a short, chubby girl. She had straight black hair that she always wore in a ponytail. She was becoming Nicky's best friend.

"Can you go with me to the corner store? Granny won't let me go that far by myself. She said I can go if you go with me, since I'm not as familiar with the neighborhood and stores like you are."

Just then Claire yelled from her room, "Who's at the door?"

"It's Molly, Mum. Can I-I go with her to the corner store?"

" Yes, but don't be gone long."

"Thanks, Mum!" He turned to Molly, " Let me g-g-grab m-my new jacket." He put the old thrift store jacket on and headed out the door.

"Gee, Nicky, that's an old coat."

"Yeah. Isn't it c-c-o-o-o-l? I bought it at the Goodmart for my b-birthday. Just look at these b-big pockets. I can really put a lot of things in them."

The two of them started walking toward the small shopping center. It was less than a mile walk, but both Nicky and Molly knew they had to be home before dark.

Molly began skipping and humming. She loved to shop and buy things just as much as Nicky. Soon she was several yards ahead of him.

"Slow down, M-Molly" Nicky yelled, as he limped faster to try to keep up.

"Alright," he heard Molly respond. She stopped next to a row of Palo Verde trees that grew along the border of the sidewalk, waiting for him to catch up. Nicky sighed with relief. Molly knew he couldn't keep up with her, but in her excitement she forgot.

Without warning, a branch from one of the trees reached down and grabbed her ponytail. Molly screamed as loud as she could, "Help me, Nicky! Help me!" She began to struggle, grabbing at the tree limb, but couldn't free herself.

Nicky yelled, "I'm c-c-coming, Molly." He began walking as fast as his legs could carry him. As he moved close to Molly, he noticed the tree that held her ponytail began to move violently. Large claw–like branches opened and closed in a threatening manner. Molly kept screaming, "Help, help," as she cried and twisted and turned to try to free herself.

Nicky moved as quick as he could, sweat rolling down his face and looking terrified as he approached his friend.

"I'm c-c-coming Mo......"

Then his feet came to an abrupt halt as a very large black dog leaped in front of him and began to prowl closer and closer to Nicky. The boy saw anger and evil in the dog's red eyes. Slowly, he began to back away from the huge beast, not realizing that soon he would be pinned-up against a nearby block fence.

"Easy boy, e-e-easy.." Nicky pleaded now, as he was trapped between the fence and the dog, which looked to be the size of a small horse. The great black dog sat down in front of Nicky and began growling viciously, showing three-inch long, razor-sharp teeth, with saliva dripping from each corner of his mouth. There was a sinister darkness, an evil fog of doom surrounding its entire body. It raised up on it's hind legs as it moved its enormous head close to Nicky's face, and his body froze in terror. This massive, dangerous creature was less than one foot from him. Nicky was unable to move his arms and his legs. They felt frozen to the ground. Then he thought, *Maybe keeping very still will keep the dog from attacking me.*

His eyes searched right and left, looking for someone or something to help him. But unfortunately there was no help in sight. Molly was still screaming, but Nicky could no longer hear her. He was facing his own terrifying predicament.

The dog started moving even closer. It raised its huge head up. Now it was only a few inches from Nicky's face, and the boy could feel the dog's smelly, hot breath on his face. Feeling hopeless, he closed his eyes and awaited the dog's attack. Then, as Nicky trembled in fear, a strange thing happened. The dog stopped growling. Nicky opened his eyes. The dog moved back and began sniffing the air around Nicky's body. Its large head raised up to meet Nicky's eyes again, and this time it spoke to the boy. The frightening voice was deep and grumbling. "Where is the Elka ? Where is the KEY? The evil Cursed One must have it now! You will give it to me!"

Nicky was in shock. His eyes grew wide with confusion and fear. He was unable to comprehend what was happening. *What is going on? Dogs don't talk! What are these strange words it is saying?* he thought.

"Talk boy!" The deep voice rumbled.

Then Nicky slowly and nervously replied, "I-I-I don't know."

"Don't *LIE* to me! I know you have touched it. I can smell it!" the dog's raspy voice said.

"I r-really don't know w-w-what you want f-f-from me!" Nicky answered in a shaky voice.

The enraged dog growled louder, more saliva dripping from his mouth as he moved within an inch of the terrified boy. Nicky cowed down in even more horror, barely able to breathe.

Just as he was sure he would be eaten, a car horn honked, and a police siren blared. Nicky, still petrified with fear, did not hear anything. But the loud noises startled the huge dog, and he paused in mid-stride.

The car pulled over and stopped near the sidewalk about ten feet from them. Nicky's eyes shifted from the dog to the car and back to the dog, his feet still frozen to the ground. The car door slammed, and a voice yelled, "Hey, Nick! Are you ok?" Montoya pulled out his gun and walked with great caution toward the boy and the dog. The scary beast quickly backed down, growled to Nicky, "I will be back," turned and ran down the street. Nicky's stress level began to drop, and he could breathe easily again. It was his friend, Officer Montoya.

He approached Nicky with his pistol in his hand. The sight of the gun in the officer's hand made Nicky realize even more the seriousness of his encounter with the large black dog.

"What's going on? That dog almost attacked you."

"Yeah, he j-just came out of no-nowhere." Nicky gave a sigh of relief, which lasted for only a brief moment. Then horror showed once more on his face.

"Oh, Monty, I'm so glad you're here. I forgot about M-Molly. She was stuck to a tree limb. We have to h-h-help her!"

"What are you talking about, Nicky?" Officer Montoya asked with a confused look.

"Nicky, Nicky" Molly came running toward them, crying.

"I'm sorry, Molly. I couldn't help you. There was this b-big dog!"

"I think I'm okay," Molly said in a sobbing voice. "I still have my ponytail, but I want to go back to my Granny's. I don't want to go to the store any more." Poor Molly seemed so upset and worn out. "I just want to go home," she said, sniffling and trying not to sob in front the officer.

Office Montoya, seeing the distress both children were in, offered them a ride home.

"Something told me that I should drive down this

street today as I was going home from patrol. This is not my usual route. I only come this way during my turn at the Neighborhood Watch."

"We are g-glad you did", Nicky said in a relieved voice.

It was a short trip to Cactus Flower Lane. The car pulled up in front of Nicky's house. Molly seemed to have calmed down some, but her eyes were still red and watery. She opened the back door and jumped out.

"Thanks for the ride, Officer. I'll talk to you later, Nicky." She turned and ran to her grandmother's house.

Nicky, still very upset, in slow motion, stepped out of the car.

"Thanks for the ride."

"Nicky, maybe I should talk to your Mom about the dog incident."

"Monty, no, you don't understand." Nicky pleaded.

"Nicky, I'll see if Animal Control can catch him, before he hurts someone."

"He is after m-me. He talked to me. I-I mean words. Some strange words, but I-I could n-not understand him!"

Officer Montoya gave a look of concern and disbelief. "I should talk to your mom. I can see you are still very shaken."

Nicky hung his head. He knew his friend Monty didn't

believe him. *What should he do?* he thought. *Everyone makes fun of me and thinks I'm weird.* He began mulling it over in his mind. *No one will believe me. Maybe I...I just thought he talked. Maybe it was the way he growled. I must have dreamed it. He didn't talk. I guess I was just scared. Yea, just scared.*

He felt a little relieved now as he took the house key out of his jeans pocket. He heard Punkin bark, "Hey, girl it's me," then he opened the door and hollered, "Mum, I'm home."

Claire was in the den, cleaning.

"You're home already?" she shouted back.

"Yeah, and I brought someone with me."

Claire hurried out to the kitchen. Punkin was sitting, glaring at the tall stranger at first, but sensing his kindness, she didn't growl. There, next to Nicky, stood a handsome, dark-haired police officer. Claire stopped and stared for a minute, then she held out her hand.

"I'm Claire Kirkland."

The officer shook her hand and introduced himself. " I'm Mike Montoya. But Nicky calls me Monty."

"Oh , you're the police officer that Nicky has spoken of. It's nice to finally meet you. Thank you for being so kind to my son. We haven't lived here very long and it's been difficult for him to adjust to new people."

"No problem, Mrs. Kirkland. That's why I'm here. It seems a large, stray dog cornered Nicky, but I was able to scare it away before it could harm him. I think he is still a little traumatized."

Claire walked over and gave Nicky a big hug. "Are you okay?"

"Yeah, Mum. I think I'll go in the den and play a video game now. Thanks for h-h-helping me, Monty. See ya." Nicky walked backed to the tiny den with Punkin on his heels.

"I'm a little worried about Nicky. He thinks this dog is after him. He said it talked to him."

"Really?" Claire replied perplexed. "He has such an active imagination. He spends a lot of time alone. He recently became interested in magic and dragons, so you will have to forgive him."

"This might not be any of my business, but where is Nicky's father?" The officer inquired.

"His father died four years ago, in the same car accident that badly injured Nicky's head and leg. It happened on his sixth birthday. Nicky was in a coma for four days. When he became conscious, he kept asking for his daddy, but it took me three weeks to tell him the bad news. I didn't want him to remember his birthday that way.

"After several months of grieving and therapy, the doctor suggested that I get Nicky a dog. He said it would help with Nicky's recovery. So we went to the Animal Rescue and picked-out a dog that was a border collie mix. He wanted to name her Pumpkin, but with his speech difficulty from the head injury, it came out Punkin.

"At first, school was difficult for Nicky, because he had missed an entire year. But it has gotten much better. Unfortunately, being harassed and made-fun-of never changes. I decided to move him, so we could start over...and here we are."

"I'm sorry to hear that. But you are doing a good job. He is a good kid."

"Thanks," Claire said as she smiled at Officer Montoya.

"Well, I must be on my way.

"I just want to tell you again, how much I appreciate you bringing Nicky home."

"Sure, any time" Montoya responded

Claire escorted him to the door

"It was very nice meeting you, Mrs. Kirkland." Montoya turned to leave, then stopped. "Oh...I have a card with my number on it." He handed his card to Claire. "If you or Nicky need my help, please feel free to call me. I work with the highway patrol, but I also do this Neighborhood's Watch."

She took the card from his hand. "Thanks." Claire smiled again as she closed the door, knowing that Nicky had a good friend in Officer Montoya. She looked at the card and attached it to the refrigerator door with a magnet.

Nicky went to bed early that night. Claire opened his bedroom door and peeked in. She hoped that he was okay. It was rare for him go to bed without saying good-night. She hesitated for a moment thinking that she would never stop worrying about him. Then she retired for the night.

That night Nicky barely slept, tossing and turning as he dreamt of the huge dog and its deep scary voice, demanding something he never heard of. *The Elka... Boy! Give me the Key!* Then he dreamt that something on top of his dresser was glowing yellow. He awoke with a start. Jumped out of bed, and walked over to his dresser, and with tired, squinty eyes scanned the top, but all he saw lying there were the rocks he had taken out of the pockets of that old jacket. He shook his head and went back to bed. *What was happening to him*? He tried to go back to sleep, and just before dawn his heavy eyelids closed and he fell asleep.

Outside of the living room window behind a bush, Der-rex stood watch. He would need more help to protect the Elka and the young human. Today he had summoned the unknowing Officer Montoya to drive down the street where Nicky was cornered by the large dog. He knew the officer would help Nicky.

But Der-rex was growing impatient, awaiting the appearance of the Sentinels and anticipating Brin-dah's return. He wasn't sure that Officer Montoya would be able to help again, if the Evil One sent his sorcerers. The human had no supernatural powers. He could not defend the boy or protect the Key without magic. And Der-rex was afraid that he alone would not be powerful enough to protect both against the ever increasing *evil* that was lurking nearby.

CHAPTER 6

WREN

Brin-dah flew on the wind and through time. It was with great urgency that she seek an audience with the Grand Glymirra. She had found the mortal child that had been foretold by the Reflection of Ages.

She would bring the Sentinel hawks back to guard and protect Nicky. She knew that the evil would appear once the boy had retrieved the Elka. The Elka must be returned to the altar before the Evil One could seize it to restore the balance. Gaeya was getting out of control in the future. Earthquakes, hurricanes, tsunamis, and lightening fires were ravaging the land and causing loss of life, not only for humans, but also for the animal and plant kingdoms.

The Fae-ren soon arrived at the outside of the Veil, the invisible sheath that hides Wren from the rest of the world.

With a wave of her hand, it parted, and she entered the outer perimeter of the realm. There, she was met by the guard Kendar, a rare, white-winged centaur. Kendar bowed his head and greeted Brin-dah. With his golden staff raised, he led the Fae-ren down the cobblestone path toward the gates of the inner Realm of Wren where many animals and birds lived and where the Grand Glymirra's sanctuary was located.

As the two of them proceeded, Brin-dah reflected on how much she missed Wren. This place had been her home since her creation. Smiling, she called to mind how this secret realm is the happiest, most beautiful, and most peaceful place that exists. As Kendar cantered and the Fae-ren floated next to him on the path, they passed several large, ancient oak and redwood trees that towered into the sky. Next to these trees were fields and fields of enormous, radiant, blooming flowers of every color of the rainbow as far as one could see. Brin-dah smiled and took in a deep breath. She appreciated the wonderful aromas of the lilacs and roses that grew near the places she drifted past.

As the pair advanced closer to the gates, the trees became smaller, and fruit could be seen hanging from apple and pear trees that lined the path to inner Wren. As she passed an apple tree, she stopped for a very brief moment to pick two apples from the tree and put them into the pocket of her toga.

The two continued down the path, spying the large stone columns in the distance that signified the entrance. Many species of plants, animals and birds that no longer lived on Gaeya Proper, lived happy and carefree here behind the Veil. Since Mortals had brought many of these great creations to extinction, they were never permitted to come into the Inner Realm under any circumstance.

However, as the populations grew, the Fae-rens could not always protect all of Gaeya without help. During periods of great need, a Guardian was chosen to enter behind the veil into the outer circle of Wren to pass important information to Glymirra. The Guardian was a mortal that Glymirra considered trustworthy and would help protect the secrets of the two worlds. This person was given a special gold opulan that could open the portals between the realms. It looked so much like a pocket watch to the Guardians that they named it the Gold Watch of Wren.

When Kendar and Brin-dah reached the entrance of the Inner Realm, Kendar bowed his head once more toward her and said, "I will leave you now." She stood in front of a huge gold and jeweled gate, twenty-five feet tall. It was flanked by the tall stone columns she had seen in the distance. With a wave of her hand, the gate opened.

As she entered the perimeter of Inner Wren, she noticed many Fae-rens scurrying around. They seemed to be confused and upset. Many winged animals were flying about, even running into one another. Feathers were flying everywhere. A giant mastodon was running so fast that it tripped over a small dinosaur, rolled, and knocked down several other animals and a marble column. A Protector Fae-ren hurried to the spot and quickly repaired the column and raised up the fallen mastodon with her powers. Brin-dah did not know what to make of all the confusion. *What was going on?* she thought to herself.

A few minutes later she arrived at the entrance of Glymirra's Sanctuary. As she passed another large marble column, a small Fae-ren helper named Tan-nah called out to her. She was a great admirer of the Protector Fae-ren, but Brin-dah did not acknowledge her. She was too focused on her mission, preparing to announce herself to the guard.

The guard, a rather small Pterodactyl named Tordawn, stood at the entrance of the Sanctuary. Though he was a guard, he harbored no weapons. His sole purpose was to announce anyone who sought Glymirra's council. No weapons were held by any guards in Wren, as this was a non-violent domain. Magic was used, but only as a source of aid or assistance.

Tordawn saw Brin-dah approach. "You have returned," he said in a surprised and excited voice.

"Yes. I seek council with the Glorious and Grand Glymirra."

As Tordawn turned to enter the over crowded courtyard of the Grand One's sanctuary, Brin-dah followed him, looking very puzzled and asked the pterodactyl, "What is all the commotion? In ten millenniums, I have not seen such chaos here."

Tordawn turned back to face her. "It's the new Evil One. His dark powers have grown stronger in such a short time, causing all of Wren to worry."

"But why? Glymirra's powers are greater! We have nothing to fear."

"You do not understand. The growing Evil and the lack of environmental balance is increasing, causing more and more destruction. More Protector Fae-rens are being sent to aid and rescue more animals. The Evil One must know this is and has been honing in on such disasters. During your absence, two of the woodland Fae-rens were attacked. They had transformed into two large elk, to lead a group of smaller animals to higher ground during a bad storm that caused much flooding. They completed their mission, but, before they could return to Wren, they were ambushed by the Evil One's sorcerers. One was able to turn back into his true Fae-ren form in time, but the other one, still in the form of an elk, was destroyed by a bolt of lightening that flew out of the sorcerer's fingers. The wizards gave a message to the surviving Fae-ren to deliver to Glymirra. He said that if The Keys are not given to the Evil Cursed One, then the Evil One and his wicked followers will enter behind the Veil and invade Wren, destroying all in their path.

Not long after that incident, two sea Fae-rens had transformed into mermaids to assist several whales that were stranded on a beach, when the tide unexpectedly went out to sea. But, they, too, were attacked by an evil sorcerer during their task. One Fae-ren was saved because he had quickly changed back to his spirit form, but his mate was destroyed by the lightening of another evil wizard. The survivor Fae-ren was given the same message: give-up the keys or they will overtake Wren.

"We both know that in all the millenia of Gaeya only one Fae-ren has ever been attacked and destroyed, that was during the mortals' great war, when all of us faced another dangerous evil. Every creature here is frightened. Upon hearing of these events, the Grand One alerted all the inhabitants of Wren to be vigilant and let her know if any strange creatures or feelings of gloom have entered Wren."

"But that's impossible! No evil can enter here! This realm is protected by powerful magic! It cannot fall against the dark! And soon, Der-rex and I will have the Elka. Then Grand Glymirra can set the balance once more. That will weaken this Evil One. That is why I am here. I need some of the gray hawks to guard the human child and help us return the Elka. Please present me to her as soon as possible. You know my mission is of great importance."

Tordawn left Brin-dah and began his approach toward Glymirra.

CHAPTER 7

THE GRAND ONE'S COUNCIL

Brin-dah stood at the opening of the large courtyard where Glymirra was giving council, and awaited her turn to speak to the Grand One. She looked on with great admiration at the rather large, majestic ruler with the body, talons and wings of a white eagle and the head and facial features of a giant human with arm-like appendages that extended out from under her massive wings. Her large blue eyes were very penetrating as she talked. It was as if she could read everyone's mind. She was perched on a long marble bench. Her wisdom was sought daily by all that lived in and out of Wren, with the exception of humans. There were many, many creatures large and small waiting. It seemed that almost all the creatures of the realm needed her wisdom and reassurance at this time.

Tordawn, realizing the great importance of Brin-dah's

request, started walking toward Glymirra. Seeing him draw near, the large eagle-like sovereign raised her large hand up, and he immediately stopped.

Using a calm, soothing voice, the Grand One spoke "Brin-dah, you may approach. I have anticipated your arrival. It is with great delight that you have come at this time."

Brin-dah stepped forward and bowed her head, then told Glymirra of finding the young boy destined to recover the Elka. Before she could request the sentinels, the ruler quietly spoke again.

"Let us retire to my inner sanctuary. We need to talk in private. I do not want to upset the realm further."

Glymirra stepped down from the perch and escorted a serious looking Brin-dah inside. As they moved toward the inner haven, Brin-dah began telling the Grand one that she and Der-rex were awaiting the young boy's recovery of the Key and that she had to hurry back to protect all. The evil was growing and may already be aware of the young boy's role in recovering the Elka.

The Grand One pointed to a marble bench, "Please sit down, Brin-dah," Then she perched herself on an adjacent marble benched.

Brin-dah ,in awe of the ruler, spoke with her head bowed,

"Please, Grand One, Der-rex and I need your help. We request the Sentinel Hawks to guard the young one, while he obtains the Elka."

"You may have all the help you need," Glymirra said. "But you must hurry, Brin-dah. For too long, Gaeya has been out of balance, and it is affecting our Realm, which is in great need of peace."

"But the evil ones cannot open the veil and enter Wren" Brin-dah boasted.

" I do not believe so. But there is a great secret that only I know. It was told to me by the Supreme of The Universe when I was presented with the Keys. This must never be whispered again. Do you understand my Fae-ren?" Brin-dah nodded. " As Her protector, it is imperative that I bring balance to Gaeya very soon. Since we are in harmony with Her, if She is destroyed, Wren will no longer exist. All other creatures will be helpless, and Evil will prevail."

Brin-dah was speechless, her immense shock causing her to freeze temporarily. Then she uttered, "Wren will be destroyed, too?"

"I must ask you again not to reveal this even to your mate. One thing in our favor is that no evil can penetrate the Veil. The threats that were made will not come true unless, by chance, they gain an opulan and can find a portal to enter. Since that likelihood is almost impossible, I am not too concerned at this time." She continued and smiled as she spoke, "The Evil would have to find a portal first, for only I know where all the portals are and when they will open to the doorway. However, my powers and the Keys' powers have never been tested in this way against such dark, dark power. The creatures of Wren have never known violence. This Realm has lived in peace since its origin.

"My concern grows from the animals on Gaeya. They tell me that the Evil One may know some of the secrets of the Fae-rens. They think it is how he was able to send his sorcerers to attack and destroy two of my Fae-rens."

"But how could he know? Maybe it was just a coincidence. Since we protect, he must be looking for disasters that would enlist our help."

Glymirra thought for a few moments, then she spoke with great care, "I cannot be sure that he only guessed at some of our secrets. We must be on alert and very careful. All the keys must be placed into their respective places within the altar very soon or all that is good could be extinguished. Now, you must go. Protect the boy, and bring me the Elka."

Bowing again, Brin-dah thanked Glymirra. As she

hurried through Wren, young Tan-nah once again tried to speak to Brin-dah, but in her haste, she passed by without noticing the other Fae-ren. She touched her orb, clasped her hands and with a blink of her eyes, she disappeared from sight, taking with her two mighty Sentinels to guard Nicky.

The three of them flew on the wind through space and time. They were trying to return before Nicky retrieved the Key. Brin-dah would have to tell Der-rex of the new dangers they faced. They must reclaim the Elka at once. The Evil One must never be able to possess even one Key, especially this one, for not even the evil would survive such a catastrophe.

The two large gray hawks, and the Fae-ren arrived at the back side of the Kirkland's' home. It was almost morning; a tiny bit of orange sun could be seen rising in the eastern sky. Der-rex greeted the three of them. He looked exhausted.

"I am very glad to see you. The evil has arrived. It is nearby."

"Yes, Der-rex, I can feel it's ghastly cold. Der-rex, we need to return the Elka as soon as the young mortal gets possession of it. All must be protected. The entire Realm is in chaos! I have never seen such fear in Wren!"

Der-rex looked perplexed at Brin-dah. Then she explained the attacks against the Fae-rens and the threats made to Glymirra regarding Wren. Der-rex shivered at the thought of evil entering behind the veil, destroying their peaceful, beautiful world.

He looked into Brin-dah's eyes and spoke, shaking off his anxiety, " The young one already has the Elka. It is in his dwelling. We must hurry to retrieve it. He has already been approached by a bewitched animal. The Evil One must have sent it. Since my powers are limited when it comes to humans, I did as you suggested and sent the boy's friend, Officer Montoya to help him. He frightened the evil animal away...this time."

Hearing this, Brin-dah grew more upset and spoke anxiously, "We must get the Elka from the young mortal. We must get it very soon. We have to triumph!"

Der-rex half-smiled and touched Brin-dah on the shoulder.

"Then we have much work to do." The Fae-rens watched as the large, gray hawks settled on the rooftops of two taller adjacent houses. They could see for miles in any direction and warn the Fae-rens of any danger.

"Nothing can get past them," Brin-dah crowed.

Then from out of nowhere came a tiny voice, "Can I help?"

Brin-dah jumped, the tiny voice startled her. "How

did you get here?" Standing behind Brin-dah was the young Fae-ren helper she ignored in Wren.

Tan-nah shuffled her feet on the ground, hung her head and whispered, " I grabbed on to the corner of your toga, just as you touched your orb to travel. I let go and hid as soon as you reached this destination. I'm sorry, but I have always wanted to travel to this world. I can help, if you will allow me."

Brin-dah stared at Tan-nah in disbelief. Then she chose her words carefully, "Tan-nah, I know you want to help, but this is a very dangerous situation. Since you are a helper, you have no powers once you leave Wren. You cannot protect yourself or anyone else here on Gaeya. As soon as I can, I will send you back. But while you are here, you must do everything I say or face Glymirra's punishment. Do you understand?"

"Yes, Brin-dah." She said as she trembled at the thought of being banished from Wren for several years for disobeying.

"Good, I want you to stay hidden behind these bushes, until Der-rex and I return. Stay in your Fae-ren form at all times. Do not let any of the Evil One's sorcerers or bewitched animals sense you. It could mean your destruction, and it will hurt our cause. Alert us if anyone gets too close to this dwelling. We will be back soon. Der-rex and I must talk alone and search the area. We need to plan our strategy. Maybe

I can find a use for you. Remember, stay hidden. Be safe."
Tan-nah reluctantly agreed and sat down behind the bushes,
maintaining her spirit form.

Just as Der-rex and Brin-dah began to plan their strategy
to get the key from Nicky, they were interrupted by the
squawking of the sentinel hawks. The two Fae-rens saw Nicky
walk over to the neighbor's earlier. He had seemed alright.
What was going on?

CHAPTER 8

THE KIDNAPPING

Earlier that morning, Nicky woke up in his usual manner, with a face-licking from Punkin. It was a restless night. Had the events of last evening been a dream? Dogs don't talk, but the large fangs and the growling seemed very, very real. Officer Monty was upset by what looked like a possible dog attack. He had even drawn his pistol. And Molly was shaken by her hair-raising event.

Nicky arose out of bed and proceeded to the kitchen. On the fridge was a note from his mom, which read:

Please stay close to home today. I think you had enough excitement for awhile. Maybe you can invite Molly over to play some video games. Take care of Punkin. No chores today. I'll be home at 4:45.

Love You ,

MOM

He poured himself some cereal, added milk, then sat at the table and ate. Punkin followed Nicky into the den. They both sat on the floor as Nicky began to play his new Magic Star-Battle video game on his X-Box. But his mind kept wandering. He just couldn't get into his favorite game today. He was still being haunted by the large black dog's voice. It kept growling, "Where is the Elka? Where is the key?"

How could this be? he thought. *How could a dog talk and what is this Elk...a?* Maybe he should talk to Molly about what happened. She would believe him.

Nicky jumped up, looked at Punkin, and said, "Let's go see Molly, girl." He got dressed, put the leash on Punkin, grabbed his thrift store jacket, baseball cap, and keys and hurried outside.

A few minutes later he was knocking on Mrs. Grey's door. The door opened slowly and Molly peered behind it.

"Can I talk to you?" Nicky said in a pleading voice. Molly hesitated. "Please Molly, p-please."

"Oh, alright. Grandma, can I go and hang out with Nicky for a few hours?"

"Yes," a hoarse female voice replied, "but don't wander too far from home."

"Okay, Granny, see ya later." She put on her jacket and

went outside to join Nicky.

Nicky, Molly and Punkin started to walk at a very slow pace down the sidewalk, toward the small park in the housing development. They were completely unaware that two large hawks were circling above, following them. Nicky turned to Molly, and with a sorrowful expression, apologized. "Molly, I'm sorry I c-couldn't help you yesterday. I don't know w-what happened."

"It's Okay, Nicky. I know you had your own problem, but that was really scary. Like something out of a horror movie."

"Molly, I-I have to tell you something. That d-d-dog that almost attacked me, it t-talked. It...it talked to me, Molly. I know no one will believe m-me, but you have to! It r-r-really did!"

Rolling her eyes, Molly looked at Nicky with great disbelief. "Really, Molly, it...it talked to me." Nicky said with much insistence.

"Nicky, I know you were scared but dogs don't talk. Right, Punkin,?" as Molly reached down to scratch behind her ears.

"I was hoping you would believe me, Molly. I-I-I knew no one else would."

He sounded so forlorn that Molly responded, though

again, in a disbelieving voice, "Well, what did that crazy dog say?"

"He wanted something called Elk...a. He kept asking me, 'Where's the key?' I don't know w-what he's talking about. It was strange. What do you th-think, Molly?"

"First, Nicky," Molly said, "Dogs don't talk. Are you sure you didn't imagine it? I know you were really frightened. Maybe his growling just sounded like words. And even if he did talk, what is an Elk...a? I've never heard that word. Let's just drop it. It's over. Move on. Don't let your imagination carry you away, as my Granny always says."

Nicky shrugged and then nodded as the two of them walked to the small park-like area located between two massive homes in the development. They strolled over to a small picnic table and sat down. It was a beautiful, clear, cool day. Punkin came and sat down next to Molly. She knew that Molly would pet her and scratch behind her ears. Suddenly, Punkin stood up, her ears perked up and her attention focused in the distance.

"What is it, girl?" Molly asked. Then the dog began whining and barking. Nicky and Molly started looking around. They didn't see any people or other animals.

"There's nothing there, Punkin. Be quiet," Nicky scolded her. Then, before he could say another word, they were surrounded by a dark human figure wearing a black robe and holding two thick chains. Attached to one of the chains was a mountain lion and at the end of the other was an enormous black wolfhound. By this time, Punkin's barking and growling became uncontrollable. All the hair on her little body stood up and her ears flattened. Nicky and Molly were frozen with fear. Less than five feet away stood the large black dog that had cornered Nicky the day before.

"Sit, sit Punkin! I don't want them to hurt you," Nicky pleaded. The dog slowly obeyed and sat down next to Molly. Though a low, almost muffled growl seemed to be coming from her.

Then, the large black dog walked up to Nicky, baring his long, saliva dripping, teeth and glared into Nicky's eyes. With Nicky sitting, the dog's massive head was at his eye level. He spoke in his deep, growling voice, "Where is the Elka? Where is the key?"

Nicky responded in a shaky voice, "I d-d-don't know what you are t-t-talking about. Who...who are you? What are you?" But before anything else could be said, the three dark creatures were attacked from the sky by the two enormous gray hawks that had followed Nicky and Molly. Their loud squawks and flapping wings were frightening. They pecked at the animals and grabbed at the evil sorcerer with their long, sharp talons. The dark figure started to glow an ominous red color, and Nicky suddenly knew they didn't have much time to escape.

"R-run, run! Go, as f-fast as you can! Take Punkin and g-get out of here!" Nicky yelled to Molly.

Holding Punkin's leash, Molly and Punkin began to run. Nicky hobbled away as fast as he could, while all the commotion was going on. But a minute later, he looked around for Molly and Punkin. They were nowhere in sight, almost as if they had disappeared. *Where are they?* He thought. *I hope they went home.* Nicky moved farther and farther from the park, but he could still hear the birds' wings flapping and the other creatures growling. He stopped again to look around for Molly and Punkin. Not seeing them anywhere, he decided to continue on home. All of a sudden, there was nothing but complete silence. He saw one of the hawks flying in the distance and the other one was following him. It seemed to be guarding him as he hurried along the street.

Nicky's body trembled as he limped towards home. *Maybe Molly and Punkin were already at his house. They could move faster then him. Please, please, be there,* he thought.

A few minutes later, he arrived at his front door. But to

his alarm, no one was there. Nicky went as fast as he could to Mrs. Grey's house. He knocked on the door loudly. *Please be here*, he said to himself. Mrs. Grey opened the door. "Is Molly h-here?" He said, out of breath.

"No, dear. I thought she was with you," she responded.

"Ok, thanks. I'll go find her. M-M-Molly's my friend and she has m-my dog," Nicky said with a nervous voice. In a panic, he turned and hurried toward the park. *Where could Molly have gone with Punkin?* There was no trace of the girl, his dog, or the strange creatures that cornered them in the park. Then Nicky looked up and saw in the distance one of the large birds that had attacked the dark creatures. It had flown so far away that it was just a speck in the sky.

*What is going on? I'm scared. Where is Molly? Where is Punkin? Where could they b*e? He kept repeating this over and over again in his mind. Nicky was breathing heavier and heavier with every step he took. His fear became more intense. He began to tremble as he looked around for signs of Molly or Punkin. He was moving farther and farther from the housing development.

Nicky started yelling, "Molly! Punkin! Where are you?" Around the next street corner, he was met by the little brown wiener dog that he had encountered a few days earlier. The dog sat down in front of him and blocked the sidewalk. "Oh, it's j-just you. Boy, I could use a f-friend right now." Nicky said sadly. Tears running down his face, as he paced back and forth. "What am I going to d-do? I can't find M-Molly and m-my dog Punkin. I hope they're okay."

Nicky stood there rubbing his eyes. "Molly! Molly!" he yelled louder.

"Stop calling your friend, Nicky." he heard a low voice say. "The bewitched creatures will hear you! They must not find you before we can get you to safety."

Nicky looked around and realized the voice was coming from the small brown dog. "You can talk, too!" Nicky said in amazement. "I'm r-really con-confused. Animals don't t-talk. I must be going c-c-crazy. Two in two days."

"No, Nicky, you are not crazy. I am called Der-rex. I am not a dog. I am one of many magical spirits that were created to help the powerful Grand Glymirra. We protect your planet and all the living. We are called Fae-rens."

An eagerness to understand overcame Nicky, along with a sense of relief that at least this dog wasn't trying to eat him. "So, you're m-magic! I knew it! There really is m-magic! Who's Glama or whoever you said ?"

"She is the care taker of Gaeya--what you call your Earth.

I was sent here to help and protect you. There is a great evil coming, and we must stop it together. You have a very special, magical key that will help us to stop this sinister darkness from progressing by returning the balance to this planet. It is the only way. The Evil One himself is trying to take this Key from you and will use any means, including kidnapping your friends. The dark sorcerer and the possessed creatures that cornered you in the park were sent by the Evil One."

Suddenly, Nicky was tired and scared again. "So this isn't a j-j-joke? Molly's not hiding from me?"

"No," the small dog responded. "I am truly sorry, but we will get them back. They are holding your friend and your dog for the Evil One. He will use them to bargain for the Elka. You must not give it to him. If the key is not restored soon to Gaeya's altar, the terrible things happening to your earth: floods, great fires, earthquakes, and tsunamis, will get much worse. Multitudes of living things will be destroyed. What is left of Gaeya will be at the hands of GREAT EVIL. We must stop this unstable environment, before it's too late."

"You said the key. What is this th-thing the dog says I have, this Elk...a?" Nicky said as he glanced at the little dog with a puzzled expression.

"The Elka is one of the Keys of Being, given to Grand

Glymmira, The Keeper of the Realm, to maintain the balance of all that is living. It is the Key of Healing. It gives new life to the living and restores order. It is very powerful."

"Why does everyone think I...I have this...this key?"Nicky responded, looking baffled.

"It was in that old jacket you are wearing, tucked away for more than seventy years, in a chest of wood and iron."

"All I found in this old coat were some r-r-rocks." Nicky said with confidence.

"Did you look carefully at all the rocks? " asked the dog.

Nicky shrugged. "I guess. They twinkled like d-diamonds"

"The Elka may look like a rock at first glance, but it is much, much more. The Elka is a dark yellow, clear stone. Your kind would call it amber. It is triangular in shape with a tiny leaf in the center. It was created from the sap of an ancient tree. You must have it. I can see you have touched it. I see your glow."

"That's silly, I'm not g-glowing. Ugh! Why am I talking to a d-dog about this?"

"I don't have much time to explain. Humans cannot see us in our spirit form, so we can change into other living creatures when needed. However, our powers are limited when it comes to people, so Brin-dah, another Fae-ren, is seeking help. One of our Sentinels, the gray hawk you saw, told me that the creatures are heading to a place you humans called Black Spirit Butte. I am here to tell you that you must go home. The Sentinels will keep you safe, and your house is the best place for you to be. Hurry! The hawks, they will guard you. I must go now and let Brin-dah know where they are taking your friends."

"I have to find them. It's my f-f-fault they were taken. I've got to find them. I don't want them to get h-hurt because of m-me." Nicky put his head in his hands and sobbed. "I can't go home without them!"

"You must go home! You must go now! You will be protected there. I will join Brin-dah, so we can get your friends back. You must listen to me or the Evil One will see you are vulnerable." Der-rex said sternly.

Nicky returned to his home as Der-rex had directed him. He sat in the dining room still dressed in his jacket and cap. He was so upset. Lying his head down on the table, he began to cry. *I have to do something, I can't just sit here while my friend and my dog are in danger.* he thought. "But what c-c-can I do?" he shouted out loud.

Then it came to him, and he jumped up from the chair and hurried into his bedroom. Nicky walked over to the dresser where he had laid the rocks from the old jacket. He picked up the first one and turned it over and over, examining it closely. It was white, with diamond-like sparkles, but it was not a small yellowish-brown stone with a leaf in the center. He set it on top of his dresser. He examined all the other stones one by one, looking for the amber one. They all looked the same to him. He didn't know what to do. He shook his head side to side in utter disappointment.

The boy gave the rocks a final look. To his surprise a small dark, yellow-amber, triangular stone with a tiny leaf in the center lay in the middle of the quartz rocks. It was actually shaped like a small prism. Nicky smiled and immediately grabbed the amber stone and put it in the front pocket of his jeans. "I will trade this triangle thing for M-Molly and Punkin".

He opened the top drawer of his dresser, pulled out his velcro wallet and placed it in his back pocket. He would need money for the bus to get to Black Spirit Butte. He went to the kitchen and wrote a note, which read:

Mom, going to get Molly and Punkin. Don't worry. Be home soon.

Love,

Nicky

Eager to get going, the boy tacked the note to the fridge and grabbed a flashlight out of the utility drawer, since it would be dark soon. Then he proceeded with great stealth out the door, tiptoeing as he went. He had to sneak past the Sentinels first. They would stop him from leaving if they caught him outdoors. Although maybe they wouldn't notice him, as they would be concentrating more on keeping the evil ones away from Nicky.

It took the boy several minutes to maneuver around the houses unseen, hiding behind bushes and block fences as he, with caution, made his way out of the housing development and to the next street. Then he hobbled as fast as he could to the bus stop, hoping a bus would be there soon. It was five miles to Black Spirit Butte. The bus could take him most of the way. He had to hurry. But unknown to Nicky, a small Fae-ren hiding behind a bush near the house next to the street, spotted him and alerted Brin-dah telepathically.

Nicky boarded the bus, paid the fare, and then sat in the empty seat directly behind the bus driver. He wanted to be ready to depart the bus as fast as he could. Black Spirit Butte was the third stop.

CHAPTER 9

NICKY'S NOTE

Claire arrived home at 4:40 pm. She unlocked the door and shouted, "I'm home!" She took off her jacket and threw it over one of the kitchen chairs. She stopped and looked around, but no one was there. *Where are Nicky and Punkin?* She turned, walked down the hall, and then went to look around the kitchen again. Then she saw the note on the fridge. *Why is Nicky going to get Molly and Punkin? What is going on?*

Just then the phone rang. Claire ran over and picked it up. "Hi, Mrs. Grey. You say that Nicky stopped about twenty minutes ago looking for Molly? I know you're worried, Mrs. Grey, so am I. It's not like Nicky to take off like this. Molly's missing. Punkin's missing. It looks like Nicky has gone to look for them. Yes, Mrs. Grey I understand. Now I am very concerned, too. I think I will call the police. I'll call you back as soon as I know something. Let me go now so I can call the neighborhood watch officer."

Claire grabbed Officer Montoya's number off of the refrigerator door. She nervously dialed the number, then paced back and forth as the phone rang a sixth time. *Why is Nicky looking for Molly and Punkin? What could have happened?*

"Montoya speaking."

"Hello, Officer Montoya, I mean, Michael, this is Claire Kirkland, Nicky's Mom. I'm calling, because the neighbor girl, Molly, is missing, and Nicky left me a note saying he was going to find her. Can you help me? It will be dark soon, and I'm really worried about the kids. Too many strange things have been happening in the last few days. I just know something is wrong."

"Sure, ma'am. I'm in the cruiser. I'll just turn around and head over to your house now," responded Montoya. "My E.T.A. is six minutes."

The officer was lost in thought, trying to think of places that Nicky and Molly may have gone. Logically, he didn't see anything bad happening to them. This was always a quiet neighborhood, where everyone looked after everyone else. However, with Nicky's close encounter with the large vicious dog that almost attacked him, and other strange occurrences, his gut told him something more must be going on.

As he was turning into Nicky's neighborhood, Officer Montoya was greatly surprised to see a blond female officer, just all of a sudden appear in the seat next to him. He swerved, almost hitting the cement curb. The tires squealed as he slammed on the brakes and abruptly stopped the vehicle.

"Where in the world did you come from? How did you get in my car? And who are you?" Brin-dah forgot that humans were so skittish. She realized she would have to calm his agitation, so he would be able to take in what she needed to tell him. She placed her hand on Montoya's shoulder. He felt an immediate peace go through his entire body. He never felt so relaxed in his life.

She told him in a soft voice, " I need you to be quiet and listen quickly. It's very important.

"I understand you may not believe me, as humans have lost touch with the other realms. I came from a land called Wren, which is behind the invisible veil between the worlds. I am a magical spirit, called a Fae-ren. I have been sitting next to you since you left that highway accident, in my true form, invisible to human eyes. I heard you talking to Nicky's mother. I was also alerted a few moments ago, by another one of my kind, that Nicky has left the protection of his home. I think he may be trying to rescue his dog and his young friend. They have been kidnapped by the Evil One's sorcerer and his bewitched animals."

"Wait, What?! How do you know Nicky? What do you mean.....*KIDNAPPED, BY WHAT*?"

"The black dog that cornered Nicky the other day was sent by an evil sorcerer. He wants something that Nicky found."

With a shocked look on his face once more, officer Montoya asked , "But how do you.... know about that big dog?"

"I am called Brin-dah. I am of the Fae-ren race. We were created to maintain the balance of your realm, your world. Another Fae-ren spirit summoned you to drive down that street where Nicky was threatened. He knew you would help the boy. Nicky is very important, and the Evil One must not reach him. That large black dog was only one of many enchanted creatures that could hurt him."

The cruiser pulled up in front of the Kirkland home.

"I will explain more to both you and Mrs. Kirkland, but we must hurry. Nicky and his friends are in grave danger."

Claire was pacing back and forth in the kitchen, wringing her hands and stopping to look out the window. She was anxious for Officer Montoya to arrive. When she saw the police cruiser pull up, she rushed out the door to meet him.

"I'm so worried, I just don't know what to do," she told the Officer. "First, that big dog corners Nicky and now Molly, Nicky and Punkin are all missing! Nicky left a note saying he was going to get Molly. I don't understand. I thought Nicky and Punkin were *with* Molly! What is going on, Michael!? I'm so glad you brought another officer to help. Please, come in."

"Thank you for your kindness, however, I cannot," the woman officer responded. "I am not human and will turn to stone if I enter your dwelling." Claire looked at Brin-dah in disbelief. *Is this woman crazy*, she thought to herself.

"Uh...what's going on? Is she serious?"

Montoya piped in, "Oh, Claire, this is Brin-dah. She says she can help us find Nicky and has a lot of explaining to do."

"Is this some kind of a...joke?" Claire asked. "It's...not... funny. I'm really, really worried about the kids!"

"Let me show you, Mrs. Kirkland," with a blink of an eye Brin-dah changed from the police officer to the young, red-haired homeless woman wearing a yellow t-shirt and torn jeans.

Claire's eyes widened. "What? That...was...you outside Walt's store the other day," she said with some skepticism. Michael Montoya blinked several times, trying to understand what had just occurred. Seeing the confused look on both of their faces, Brin-dah began to explain.

"Mrs. Kirkland, Officer Montoya, I know why Nicky has been experiencing strange and perilous incidents. I know where he is going and what the Evil One is searching for. For you to understand what is going on and the dangers involved, I must tell you about my realm, the magical world behind the veil of Wren and what changes have taken place in your world in the last seventy human years.

"My kind, Fae-rens, were created to help the Grand Glymirra keep the balance of your realm, or what you call your world. We have existed alongside humans from the beginning. We were given special powers of our own, so we are able to change into any living creature in order to protect. Human beings are the only living creatures that cannot see us in our true form. As I told Office Montoya, we are spirits, and we are limited when it comes to helping your kind.

"For thousands of years, this realm that we call Gaeya, your Earth, lived in peace and harmony. Then humans appeared. The Supreme of the Universe was proud of these new creatures, until they soon multiplied into a violent and greedy species. Seeing the great chaos and destruction they caused, He gave our ruler, the Grand Glymirra, also known as the Keeper of the Balance, the Keys of Being. These Keys control the elements and bring about healing and rebirth of this world when needed. The Keys would keep humans from controlling everything.

"For thousands of years, humans have fought to control each other, and we, the protectors, took care of all the non-human creatures and plants, living above and below the seas. Powerful Glymirra was able to keep the balance. Then humans invented weapons that could not only destroy each other but also the terrain and other living creatures. This greatly worried Glymirra, because the destruction was altering the balance, leaving your realm vulnerable. As long as the elements were still under Glymirra's control , she could protect all other living creatures. As your weapons became more highly developed, and the Major War of your realm in your year 1918 ended, Glymirra decided to send several Fae-rens to spy on leaders all over your world.

"Then in 1941, two years into your World War II, a leader named Hitler, with the aid of evil sorcerers, realized that controlling the elements would give him power over all that lived. So, with the help of the darkest magic known, he began his quest to find the source of balance and throw your world into a chaos that only he could control. Glymirra sent her most trusted, most clever and most powerful leader of the Fae-rens,

Phan-non, to watch the encampment of Hitler.

"As days passed, Phan-non decided that he needed to get closer, so he transformed into a German guard and posted himself in front of the Headquarters' door, not knowing that Hitler had sent for three of the most powerful sorcerers of your world. You see, great evil can sometimes sense our presence because Fae-rens have an aura of goodness that can be felt no matter what form we take.

"When our great Phan-non was discovered spying on Hitler, the sorcerers destroyed him before he could change back into his spirit form. We are more vulnerable in another form, because our powers weaken. The act of extinguishing his aura alerted Glymirra that he was no more, and she needed to protect the Keys of Being from such immense darkness.

"Glymirra called for me and Der-rex, my mate. We are the Protector Fae-rens. She asked us to take the Keys of Being that were kept in a deep underground grotto in the Altar of Hope and hide them in far away lands, so that no one could find them, even Glymirra. So Der-rex and I were given the four wooden boxes, each containing a key and sealed with the golden wings of her symbol. These boxes were enchanted with additional incantations so that it might aid in concealing them. We set out to hide them, from all the evil and destruction.

"Each key was then hidden in a remote location in various times and protected with many special enchantments. After the fall of Hitler, and the Great War ended, Glymirra sent us to retrieve the Keys so that she could return them to the Altar of Hope. The land and its creatures had much healing to do. It would need both Glymirra's and the Keys' great powers to restore the balance.

"So, in the autumn of your year 1945, Der-rex and I set out to collect the Keys, only to find that the last and most powerful of them had been accidentally discovered and moved. We were devastated. After consulting the Reflection of Ages, a crystal that shows the past and tells the future, it was revealed to the Grand Glymirra that a young mortal boy, unaware of the Key's great powers, had taken it from the branch of the Ancient Oak tree. It was then foretold that another young mortal boy in a far off desert land, in the tomorrow world, would retrieve the Elka, the Key.

"We were sent to find him and bring back the Elka, in order to set the balance and weaken the Evil One's Powers. If we fail, your realm or world as you call it, could be destroyed. It may even effect our world behind the veil. We cannot save all the living. We can only try to protect.

"Our journey has been long and difficult. Only a few

years after the Great War ended, Glymirra received word that another great evil was rising. One that was stronger than the world had ever known. A Fae-ren also reported hearing the forest creatures talk about the Evil One, that he knew about the Keys and Wren. He knows that they control the elements. And, more than anything, he wants to gain control from Glymirra.

"We discovered recently that the young boy that had originally taken the key had grown old and expired from this world. It has been carried here in the wooden and iron trunk from a land you call Wales."

"So why didn't you get it from the trunk yourselves?"

"Like I said before, we are limited when it comes to humans. A Fae-ren cannot enter an occupied human dwelling. We can lose all magical powers. Also, if we touch objects made of processed iron, we will turn to stone. So even though we have powers, we also have great limitations. It's to keep us from interfering with human existence. After waiting many years, the key was moved again to this arid land."

Claire Kirkland looking very bewildered, interrupted Brin-dah, "I don't understand what Nicky has to do with this Key thing."

"Well, when Nicky purchased that old coat, he unknowingly recovered the Key, since it was hidden in one of the pockets. The Center key, the Elka is made of amber," Brin-dah turned and looked at Officer Montoya. "And your friend Nicky has it. The Evil One knows this and will do anything in his power to get the key."

Claire stood staring at Brin-dah in shock. *What will happen to my son?* she thought. *I don't know what to do.*

"We have tried to make contact and gain the boy's trust, but as the Evil grows ever stronger, it has been difficult. We hope that he will give the key, the Elka, to us and not to the Evil One. The dark sorcerer wants to use it to control all the living. He does not realize by causing chaos and destruction, it could end everything. The Balance must be restored soon. That is why your world has been experiencing an escalation of earthquakes, tsunamis, lightening fires, and volcanic eruptions. With all the advanced human communication, I am sure you have heard of such increased devastation around this planet."

Brin-dah turned to Montoya, "Now we must go to the place you call Black Spirit Butte. That is where the girl and the dog are being held. Please stay inside the house, Mrs. Kirkland. We don't want anything to happen to you, and if we meet Nicky on our way there, we will send him back. Do not be so distressed. Everyone will be returned safely to you. Once we retrieve the key, the Evil One should leave all of you alone.

"Now we must go with great haste. We must save all before the sorcerer that has taken the young girl and the dog has a chance to seek more evil help. My mate, Der-rex, will meet us at our destination."

Brin-dah changed back to the blond police officer, and she and Michael Montoya left in the patrol car with lights flashing and sirens blaring.

Claire ran to the kitchen window, pulled back the curtain and watched as the patrol car departed. She was nervous, but she would have to trust them. She knew she could not help in the rescue, and she needed to be there in case Nicky returned. But waiting and not knowing what was going on would be very difficult.

CHAPTER 10

BLACK SPIRIT BUTTE

The police cruiser pulled up to the entrance of Black Spirit Butte.

"I will leave you now. I must meet Der-rex. We will meet you at the west side of Black Spirit Butte. But hurry and be careful. We mustn't dally any longer." Brin-dah clasped her hands, and with a blink, she was gone. Officer Montoya parked the cruiser on the west side of the Butte and proceeded to meet up with the Fae-rens.

The sun had dropped below the summit and would be setting soon. Officer Montoya had to move quickly, but he was still trying to understand what was going on. *Magic Spirits, evil sorcerers, keys, rocks, was he imagining all of this?* He was concerned about the kids, and his instincts told him he needed to check it out. After all there were some strange happenings that he had witnessed in the last few days. Besides that, his young friend seemed really upset about them. *Maybe Nicky knew something he didn't.*

As he started walking toward the west side of the mountain, a sudden, warm gust of wind stopped him. Officer Montoya covered his eyes for a moment. When he looked up, a young man had appeared in front of him. "I am Der-rex, a Fae-ren like Brin-dah. We have located the opening to the cave where the dog and the girl are being held. Come with me."

With the blink of an eye, he changed from a mortal to a mountain goat. The officer stepped back and looked on in amazement. The goat looked back at him. "We must hurry," came from its mouth. Still unable to comprehend all that he had seen and heard, the officer followed close behind the animal.

A fog hung above them, layered in rings around the mountain, each layer becoming denser and denser. Der-rex led him to the west side of the mountain, which was very steep and rocky. A sign read : DANGER- HIKING PROHIBITED. There was only a partial hiking path left due to the large rock slide that occurred two years ago. It was considered too dangerous to clear and reopen.

Montoya was worried. He wasn't dressed to climb such

rough terrain and kept slipping and sliding. There was a thick fog everywhere, making it difficult to see the rocks above him. He was afraid that he would not be able to reach the cave. Reading his mind, Der-rex sent a swirl of warm wind to lift Montoya to the ledge close to the entrance of the caves. The Fae-rens joined him on the ledge.

Officer Montoya looked down and shook his head in astonishment, "I don't believe I would have made it to the ledge without your help. Thanks!"

The three discussed their rescue plan, unaware that Nicky was close behind. "We must be very careful. The Evil One will have sent one of his sinister sorcerers to commandeer the key. He knows we will try to free the young human and the dog. They will use their magic against you. The Evil One also controls many bewitched animals. You never know what will approach you. You need to proceed with great caution. We will change to our Fae-ren form. They cannot hurt us in our true form. You will not be able to see us, but we will do all we can to protect you. The evil ones, however, may be able to sense us. Let us approach the cavern quickly but with great vigilance."

Officer Montoya pulled the gun from his holster and slowly stepped forward into the cave opening. It was very dark. He had forgotten his flashlight. "Can you give me some light?" he whispered. Then a small ball of light appeared before him. It moved slowly ahead of him, stopping when he stopped and moving when he moved. The cave was very tortuous. Its path was filled with loose rocks and other rough areas where small rock slides had occurred, making it difficult to be as quiet as possible.

Then suddenly the ball of light ahead of him blinked out. Michael stopped and stood still in the dark. A strange peaceful feeling came over him. Then a voice spoke in a whisper, "We are almost there. There is a light around the next turn."

Montoya took a deep breath. *How could he approach such creatures of magic? In all his years as a cop he never dealt with the supernatural. That was just a myth. Such things were not real.* Brin-dah read his thoughts and whispered in his ear, " Do not be afraid. We will be with you."

Officer Montoya and the Fae-rens reached the opening of the cave room. Cautiously, they peeked in and looked around. Then the cop saw Molly sitting in a corner with Punkin. He did not see anyone else. The inside of the cave curved, making it hard to see if anyone else was standing around the corner. Putting one foot in front of the other in slow motion, he stepped just inside the cave and ducked behind a boulder that stood next to the entrance. He was followed by Der-rex and then by

Brin-dah, who lagged a few feet behind, both still maintaining their true Fae-ren forms. It would be more advantageous to stay invisible.

Montoya looked around the room of the cave once more. He did not see or hear anyone else. So, with a wave of his hand, he signaled that he was going to move closer to Molly and Punkin.

As he moved forward slowly, Officer Montoya was taken back by a loud roar. A six foot cougar! This was impossible! The large cat lunged in front of him, but was stopped immediately as if it had run into a wall. A deep voice could be heard coming from the shadows. It commanded, "Staydra!"

At the sound of this word, Montoya's body stiffened and he fell to the floor with a loud thud. It was like he was frozen. Just then Molly noticed him, letting out a scream at the sight of the policeman lying on the floor.

Then the raspy voice said, "I know you are here Fae-ren. Show yourself now or these mortals will pay."

In the corner Molly sat frightened. Her hands and feet were bound with dark pieces of cloth. Punkin laid next to her, confined to the corner by the large, heavy rock, which rested on the end of her leash.

Brin-dah moved back closer to the entrance, leaving

Der-rex to contend with the Evil. He appeared as the small brown dog, knowing that he was more vulnerable in this state. It was the only way to protect Brin-dah. She had to shield herself by magic, so her aura would not be sensed.

Over the years, the Evil One's sorcerers had grown more powerful. They seemed to be able to detect even the cleverest of Fae-rens. Brin-dah had never known this much fear. She must escape and get help. Der-rex never expected to be unmasked by an ordinary sorcerer. The Fae-rens did not know that these sorcerers were so powerful. Shaking and terrified, Brin-dah backed very slowly out of the cave. She must get help now.

Realizing she did not have time to seek help from Glymirra, Brin-dah clasped her hands and moved swiftly through the night, back to Nicky's house. She had to think of a way to draw the sorcerer and his evil animals away from the cave. She would have to enlist the help of the two Sentinels and maybe the young Fae-ren helper.

The Gray hawks and Tan-na received her telepathic message and were waiting for her at the Kirkland's backyard. When she arrived at Nicky's house, an idea came to her. She would turn Tan-na into a Nicky "look-a-like" and Tan-na and the hawks would draw the evil ones far south, giving Brin-dah time to rescue everyone at Black Spirit Butte. She shared the plan with the others. Then, she gave the blue orb that hung around her neck to Tan-na.

"As soon as all are free, I will let you know. You must use the orb. It will take you and the sentinels through time and back to Wren. Der-rex and I will be close behind. We will use his orb to return. Now go and be swift."

CHAPTER 11

TO THE RESCUE

Nicky boarded the bus. Black Spirit Drive was the third stop. It seemed like an eternity to an anxious Nicky before he arrived at his destination. The bus did not go all the way to the mountain. He got off the bus and stood surveying the distance to Black Spirit Butte. It was still about a half a mile walk to the old gate of the visitors trail. It had been closed for a few years due to rock slides.

Nicky had learned at school in his Native American History Class that this area had been unstable for more than a thousand years, when cliff dwellers tried to live in the caves there. Heavy black fog, rock slides and tremors made them flee the caves before they actually settled-in. Only a few partial rock walls and a few clay pots were left in the caves. Because the natives believed it was possessed by evil spirits, it was given the dark name of Black Spirit Butte. Even the scientists were stumped. No one really seemed to know why this butte had tremors and dense, dark fog all year round. No other mountain in the state displayed these ominous characteristics.

Nicky began to walk as fast as he could toward the Butte, but his left leg held him back. He wished he didn't hobble so, and he wished he could move faster. After all he needed to reach Molly and Punkin as soon as possible. *I need to move faster*, he thought. In frustration, he yelled, "Please, help me!" His pocket began to glow a bright yellow color, then a sudden swirl of warm wind surrounded him. It scared him, so he closed his eyes.

The warm wind blew hard on his body, and he felt like he was flying. He looked around and noticed that he moved very fast through the air toward his destination. A few seconds later, he stopped. A calm feeling enveloped him. When he opened his eyes, he stood at the bottom of the Black Spirit Butte, looking around in disbelief. *What had just happened?* One minute he was walking then the next minute he was standing at the bottom of the back of the Butte. *Was it magic*? He didn't know what to think, but he didn't have time to analyze it. He really had to hurry. B*ut what could he do to move faster*?

In a nervous state, he began to talk to himself, "I sure

wish I-I could r-r-run. It will t-take m-me for...forever to get to the front." Then with a whoosh a funnel of warm air lifted him up and once more he was moving on air, whipping around the base of the mountain, until he faced the front of the Butte where, high above, several cave openings where supposed to be. Nicky stood for a moment, frightened and intimidated by the massive cloud of dark fog that encircled the upper third of the butte. The sun was almost totally behind the summit, and it was becoming difficult to see.

He looked up again and spied a ledge just below the ring of fog. *That must be where the cave openings are*, he thought to himself. He was sure Molly and his dog would be in one of the caves, but how was he to get up there? Then he heard a loud rumble. The ground shook and some dirt and rocks came showering down around him. Nicky froze for a minute in fear. As soon as the ground stopped moving, he brushed some of the dirt and dust off. Now he was really frightened but had no choice but to continue. *How am I going to find them*? he thought with his body trembling.

By now it was almost dark. Nicky wasn't sure which way to go. Just then he heard a loud screaming that echoed around the mountain. It sounded like Molly. Nicky started climbing toward the sound, trying to hurry. But he kept sliding back down every time he gained a few feet. There was so much loose dirt and rocks. He was getting frustrated.

It seemed like a long way up to the ledge that would take him to the cave openings. Because of the fog surrounding the top, he could not see any way to reach the entrance of the caves. A chill came over him, and the air suddenly grew colder in the darkness. *This is really a spooky place,* Nicky thought. It was lit only by a tiny bit of light from the full moon that shined through a small hole in the circle of fog above.

He looked around, contemplating his next move. There was so much loose rock that he didn't know how he could scale the rocky side of the butte, but that is where he heard Molly's scream. He kept reminding himself that he must be quick but quiet. He would have to be careful. If he was injured, how could he help Molly and Punkin?

He looked up again at the faint ledge where the entrances to the caves must be. He whispered in frustration, "It would be great if I could fly up to the ledge." Nicky didn't notice that his pocket was glowing again, and before he could take his first step, a strong , warm gust of wind swirled around him again. This time, the wind picked him up and set him gently down on the rocky ledge in front of three cave openings.

Whoa! It's like magic! But where is it coming from?

He was puzzled, but again he did not have time to figure things out.

Which cave should I take? Nicky thought. He walked over and peeked into each opening, not sure which one to enter and follow. He didn't have much time so he had to choose the right one. Then he heard another loud scream. It was Molly. It came out of the cave opening to the far right. He was afraid for Molly, but he also felt a kind of relief to know that he would be entering the correct opening. It meant he would be there in a shorter time. He took the flash light out of his jacket pocket and turned it on. He would go into that cave and follow it to Molly and Punkin.

As he started moving through the narrow, curvy tunnel of the cave he could feel his heart pounding. The pounding grew harder and louder. In fact, it seemed so loud that he thought everyone would be able to hear it. His breathing also increased. He realized now how frightened he was and that he really didn't know what he would do once he reached them. The evil creatures could overpower him, and then he would be their prisoner! The sorcerer could cast a spell on him and turn him into something else. These ideas startled him. *How could he bargain with them*?

He came to a complete halt just before the end of the

twisty tunnel. He was in such a hurry that he almost forgot the terrible danger that he was approaching. He had to think of a way he could sneak in undetected. *The animals can smell me, the sorcerer can sense me. How can I get past them?*

He began to pace in the small tunnel area he was in and began talking to himself once more. He was so scared. " I've g-got to t-think. If only I-I was in....invisible and not smelly. I need a f-force field, like in m-my video game. No one could sense m-me or s-see me. I-I would be pr-protected. I could save Mo-Molly and P-Punkin."

Without a sound, the amber stone in his pocket glowed once more. This time, Nicky felt a slight heat radiate through his whole body. A sudden gust of very warm wind gathered around his feet. He looked down and realized that he couldn't see them. Then he looked at his hands and touched his chest. To his surprise he was invisible!

CHAPTER 12

NICKY'S ARRIVAL

As Brin-dah was turning Tan-na into a Nicky "look-a-like", the real Nicky reached the opening of the cavern where his friend and dog were held captive, unaware of how he would be able to rescue them . He stopped at the entrance of the cave, then in slow motion mode he peered inside to survey the area. Thoughts of saving Molly and Punkin kept running through his mind. *If he gave up the amber rock....this key, would they really let them go or would these evil creatures hurt them anyway?* He had seen too many movies. But he had to act now.

Nicky was ready to proceed into the cavern, but as he began to step inside, he heard a familiar voice. He immediately stopped to listen. It was Der-rex. He heard him say, "The boy, and the key are safe. The sentinels will protect him. He will not come here. You will not win!"

"Don't play games with me, Fae-ren, the Evil Cursed One will be angry. If I do not possess the Elka soon, he will come with all his wrath, and Gaeya itself will quake beneath his might. His powers are stronger than Glymirra's. They grow more and more each day. No one can escape him," the dark sorcerer sneered.

The small dog spoke with confidence, "I am telling you that the boy and the Elka are safe and protected. You will not get them."

The sorcerer's eyes widened, anger covering his face. He lifted his arm and with the wave of his hand, Der-rex was thrown with great force up against the nearby rock wall. His small body fell to the hard dirt floor, and he did not move.

Molly let out another scream and began to cry. The sorcerer only laughed as he gathered his animals.

Nicky decided that he must go inside and try to help his friends, but he must be careful. He moved in a deliberate manner and peered inside. The large room was dimly lit by two wall torches. His eyes began scanning for Der-rex, Punkin, and Molly.

He noticed the small dog on the floor, motionless. He saw

Molly and Punkin bound in a corner. Then he heard a moaning sound. Looking towards it, he realized it was his friend Monty. Officer Montoya was awakening from his frozen stupor. Nicky wanted to rush over and make sure he was okay, but he knew he must remain quiet and still. He was no match for the sorcerer or his bewitched animals. He must wait for the right time.

Monty shook his head. He needed to focus his brain and try to register what had happened. Then he saw Der-rex lying silently on the hard ground. The officer slowly sat up. He was still dazed, but he could hear Molly who was sobbing and asked her, "No one has hurt you, have they, Molly?"

She lifted her sad eyes towards him, and responded, "No, but I think he killed the little dog."

Officer Montoya looked once more to where the small dog laid lifeless. He tried to get up to go to it, but he was not able to stand up.

Nicky was upset. He didn't know that Officer Montoya was a prisoner there, too. And now Der-rex, who came to rescue them, was hurt or maybe even dead, killed by the this dark sorcerer. How was he to rescue everyone and where was the other Fae-ren? He knelt behind a nearby boulder, contemplating his next move. Nicky was still invisible. *I wish all those evil beings would leave, so I could help my friends,* he thought to himself.

Then as if someone heard his thoughts, a bright red sphere appeared in front of the sorcerer. A booming voice came out of it, alerting him that the boy and the hawk guards were seen traveling south. "You must stop him at once and bring me the Key!"

The boy heard the sorcerer speak to the creatures as they began to move toward the opening of the cavern. He was confused how they had seen him when he was here. But, it appeared they were going to leave the butte and go looking for Nicky and the Elka.

Nicky stepped just inside the cave room and hid behind the large rock that laid next to the entrance. He held his breath as the evil ones walked past him and exited the cavern room. The sorcerer's body became a red flame, and with a wave of his hand, the sinister three disappeared.

Nicky breathed a sigh of relief. He had done it. They didn't see or sense him! Then he stood up and looked around the room. He looked worried as he approached Molly. Stooping down behind her, he began to untie her. She didn't see anyone and didn't know what was happening, so she began to wiggle and fight.

"Stop, Molly, it's me." She immediately recognized her

friend's voice. "Nicky, where are you? I can't see you."

Nicky laughed, "I'm in-invisible," he announced in a loud excited voice. "Isn't it a-awesome?"

Molly had a really puzzled look on her face. "Really, Nicky? How?" she asked, as she rubbed her wrists.

"I'm not s-sure how I got this way, but the guy in the b-black cloak and his animals could not s-s-see or s-s-smell me. I came to save you and P-Punkin. I didn't kn-know that Officer M-M-Monty was here too."

Then Nicky turned toward Officer Montoya. "Can you get up okay?"

Officer Montoya was looking around. "Yes, I think so.

Nicky saw him struggling.

"Where are you, Nicky?"

" I'm walking towards you, Monty. Maybe I c-can help you g-get up."

He was still in a groggy state, so Nicky helped him up.

"Thanks," Montoya said. Nicky walked back over to Molly and helped her free Punkin's leash. Punkin stood up and shook herself, tail wagging happily. Then all of them, looking very solemn, walked over to the lifeless body of the small dog lying on the floor of the cave.

Officer Montoya reached down and slowly turned

Der-rex over, checking to see if there was anything that could be done for him. He couldn't tell if Der-rex was breathing, after all he wasn't an ordinary living creature. He was a magical creature. Molly stood there crying again. Nicky just stood, starring into space.

"This is all my-my fault. If I-I hadn't bought this stupid j-j-jacket, none of this would have happened."

Officer Montoya picked up Der-rex's body. "We have to go now. Maybe Brin-dah can help him."

Molly picked up Punkin's leash, and they all started for the opening. Officer Montoya could see a flashlight bouncing in the air and Nicky's footprints following him.

So he turned to Nicky. "I will lead the way, but I need your flashlight to see if it's clear to leave.

Montoya laid Der-rex's body down on a nearby boulder. Nicky handed the flashlight to Officer Montoya. But as soon as Montoya tried to step out of the cavern room, he was knocked back. "Whoa!" He tried again to leave, but was stopped in his tracks once more. He turned with a jerk and threw his hands up in frustration. Scowling, he said, "That evil Sorcerer has done something to the opening. We can't get out!"

Nicky walked over to the opening and touched something smooth. "It's l-l-like an invisible shield. Like in my video game.

He put a c-c-curse or dark enchantment on the o-opening."

The three of them stood there terrified. Molly was so upset, her whole body seemed to be trembling. Then she began to weep again.

"What are w-we g-going to do, Monty?" Nicky asked.

" I...have...no...idea." he responded in frustration."I don't know anything about magic or spells. I don't know what will happen if we cannot escape soon. Our only hope is Brin-dah. She left to get help when the evil sorcerer sensed Der-rex?"

"What about Der-rex" Nicky said.

The three of them looked once more at the lifeless body that lay on the boulder.

"I'm sorry, Nicky," Montoya said as he stood there shaking his head left and right. "There's nothing we can do."

CHAPTER 13

BRIN-DAH'S RETURN

Nicky, still invisible, began to pace. "I'm never gonna b-buy anything at the thrift store again. Please, Monty, think of s-something before those g-gruesome ones return. I know they w-w-want me and this weird looking key." Nicky put his hand in his pocket and touched the amber key. "Der-rex said that t-terrible things would happen if that evil guy that they w-w-work for gets his hands on it. It has great p-p-power!"

Officer Montoya, feeling extremely agitated, walked over to the opening. Using his hands, he began to feel around for any holes or small openings around the edges of the shield. He bent down and checked the bottom, too. After a few minutes, he stood up.

"It's solid," he said in a disappointed tone. "We better

hope Brin-dah comes for us soon."

Molly once again began to cry. "I'm scared."

Nicky put his invisible arm around her. "I'll protect you Molly. I-I won't let them h-h-hurt you."

Several minutes had passed. Feeling defeated, they all sat on the dirt floor, leaning up against the wall closest to the entrance. A burst of warm wind flew by them. All of a sudden, in their midst, stood Brin-dah in the form of the woman officer.

"I must get all of you out of here. We must move with great haste. The dark sorcerer and his creatures are searching for Nicky and the Elka. If they do not catch the decoy we have sent out, they will return here and send for the Evil One himself. None of us can fight him. His powers are very mighty.

"The Fae-ren helper Tan-na that came back with me, has changed into a mortal that looks like Nicky. She and the sentinels are leading the evil creatures far south. It should give us enough time to escape. Unless the sorcerer realizes he is being tricked. We must go... now!"

Just as Brin-dah finished speaking, Molly pointed to the lifeless body laying on the nearby boulder. Brin-dah looked with great sorrow and surprise. "Oh, Der-rex." She scooped up the small dog in her arms, hugging him to her.

"Is there anything you can do for him," Molly asked.

"Can you use your magic" Nicky's voice asked from behind Officer Montoya.

Looking down at Der-rex , she answered," I can try. But we become very vulnerable when we transform into other living creatures. It is how the evil can hurt or destroy us. I must get all of you out of here, but first I must take my true form. I am more powerful as a Fae-ren."

Then she stopped for a moment. "Where is Nicky? I heard his voice."

"Here I am."

"But you are invisible like me," Brin-dah stated with surprise. "You have used the Key's powers."

"What?" Nicky exclaimed.

"You have the Key in your possession. Am I right?"

"It's in my p-pocket. I thought maybe I could use it to b-bargain for M-Molly and Punkin. Then I r-r-realized, it would be wrong to give it to them. I only asked for h-help. And now I'm in-invisible. Der-rex told me that it had great p-powers."

"No human had ever used the Key's Magical powers. We Fae-rens did not know that a non-magical being could call upon the Elka's powers. You must be very special indeed, Nicky. I may need you to help me later. But now I must remove this shield."

Brin-dah turned to the opening of the cave, clasping her hands and closing her eyes she whispered "dissa." Immediately, the shield was gone.

"Everyone, the shield is no more, you can now leave. Officer Montoya, will you carry Der-rex for me?"

"Sure, Brin-dah, "he replied.

"Please, we must go now, before they realize they are chasing the wrong Nicky."

Brin-dah stopped and closed her eyes for a moment, sending a telepathic message. "I have sent word to the Fae-ren, the Nicky look-a-like and the sentinels that I have rescued all of you. They are ordered to travel back to Wren. Once they have disappeared, the sorcerer will know I tricked him."

Everyone hurried out of the cavern room and through the narrow passage as Brin-dah's ball of light lit the way. Soon, they were out of the cave and standing on the outside ledge.

"I sense that evil is nearby. Nicky hold on to me. I will need your power to help transport officer Montoya, Molly, Der-rex and your dog to safety."

Nicky held on to Brin-dah. A huge, warm funnel of wind lifted everyone and carried them swiftly back to Nicky's house.

CHAPTER 14

THE HEALING KEY

Nicky was safe but still invisible. It was hard for Claire to understand. She wanted her son back in his human form. Nicky thought it was cool, but he knew he couldn't stay this way.

After everyone was reunited and emotions seemed to settle down, Brin-dah turned to the body of Der-rex. that was laying on a wooden stool on the patio, where officer Montoya had placed him when they returned. Brin-dah used her magic and moved the stool, with the little dog's body, through the air and set it down on the small plot of grass in the Kirkland's backyard. Everyone at the Kirkland home joined the Fae-rens in the backyard.

"Nicky, I will need you to give me the Elka, for it is the Key of Healing and Rebirth."

Nicky reached into his pocket and pulled out the amber Key. He immediately returned to his human form. Claire was overjoyed to be able to see and touch Nicky again and hugged him tightly.

Brin-dah took the amber Key and placed it on top of the body of Der-rex. Then, waving her hand over him, she began to chant in an almost melodic, singing tone. Everyone stood in a big circle around the stool and watched with intense curiosity. Even Pumpkin sat in silence. Molly put her head down and folded her hands like she was praying with Brin-dah.

The key began to glow. The yellow glow grew brighter and brighter. The brightness became blinding. First, Claire covered her eyes, and then everyone was forced to cover their eyes, all except for Brin-dah. She watched with great awe and hope. Then the glow went out.

Der-rex slowly began to move. His eyes opened. Brin-dah shouted "Der-rex!" Everyone opened their eyes, looking on with amazement. They were happy to see Der-rex alive.

The little dog lifted his head, then he spoke. "I am back from the dark!" With much excitement, he changed back into his Fae-ren form.

"We must return the Elka to Glymirra. It is with great urgency that we must leave all of you. The Evil is on its way."

Placing the Elka in the pocket of her toga, Brin-dah turned to Nicky, "Now that we have the Elka, the Evil One will not harm you. Maybe when you are older, the Great Glymirra will bestow on you the honor of Guardian. You have shown all that you are trustworthy and good. Your brave and true heart have been rewarded. The Elka has healed you."

Nicky's eyes widened with surprise. He realized that Brin-dah was right. His left leg was back to normal. He jumped around in excitement.

"I don't limp any more." He ran down the sidewalk and back. "Look, Mum, I'm cured! I'm cured." Claire grabbed him and hugged him, crying tears of joy... She was so overcome, she could not speak. Her son was healed!

Nicky turned around. "Thank you, Brin-dah!"

He looked around, then he realized that the Fae-rens were gone. " They left." He ran to the other side of the house, and everyone followed him. He looked at the roof tops. It was strange not to see the hawks watching and guarding. Everything now seemed like a weird dream.

"Well, Nicky, I guess you won't be getting into any more trouble," Officer Montoya, grinned with a brow up. "I must be going."

Claire walked over next to him. "Thank you for all your

help, Michael."

"I didn't do anything. If it wasn't for Nicky and Brin-dah, we wouldn't be here. You should be very proud to have a son like Nicky."

"I am," replied Claire. She smiled and gave Nicky another hug. "I always knew you were special."

The boy looked at her and blushed, "Oh, Mum," he said with a sheepish grin.

Molly spoke up, "I bet Granny's really worried about me."

"Oh Molly, I almost forgot, I told her that I would call her as soon as I knew what was going on. She is very worried. You should hurry home now. I don't know if she will understand what happened, so if you like, I can call her later and explain."

"That would be great, Mrs. Kirkland." Molly went over to Nicky and gave him a big hug. "Thanks for saving me."

"Any time," he replied.

Then she skipped across the street to her grandmother's house, smiling, happy that everything was back to normal.

"I really need to go," officer Montoya repeated.

"Would you like to come over for dinner sometime? Nicky and I would like having a new friend."

"I would like that too," he said smiling. "You have my number. I will look forward to dinner with the two of you."

" Thank you, Monty, for believing me." Nicky said, shyly.

"Well Brin-dah was pretty convincing and too many strange things had happened to you. Take care, Nick." The officer went out to his cruiser and drove off.

"Mum, look at me run!"

Claire was ecstatic. No one would ever tease her son again. She even noticed he no longer stuttered. He had received a great gift from the amber Key.

The helper Fae-ren and the Sentinels had returned to Wren. They were met by Glymirra. Tan-na told the Grand One that Brin-dah had the Elka, and she and Der-rex would be there soon.

But time passed and the protector Fae-rens did not return...